# CRUZ

**ALSO BY THE AUTHOR**

*My Favorite Scar*

# CRUZ

## NICOLÁS FERRARO

TRANSLATED FROM THE SPANISH BY

**MALLORY N. CRAIG-KUHN**

**SOHO
CRIME**

First published in Spanish in Argentina by Editorial Revólver, 2017

Copyright © 2017 Nicolás Ferraro
English language copyright © 2022 Nicolás Ferraro

First published in English in 2022 by
Soho Press, Inc.
227 W 17th Street
New York, NY 10011

Library of Congress Cataloging-in-Publication Data

Names: Ferraro, Nicolás, author. | Craig-Kuhn, Mallory N., translator.
Title: Cruz / Nicolás Ferraro ; translated from the Spanish by Mallory N.
Craig-Kuhn. | Other titles: Cruz. English
Description: New York, NY : Soho Crime, 2022.
Identifiers: LCCN 2022003484

ISBN 978-1-64129-529-1
eISBN 978-1-64129-397-6

Subjects: LCGFT: Thrillers (Fiction) | Novels.
Classification: LCC PQ7798.416.E873 C7813 2022 | DDC
863/.7÷dc23/eng/20220209
LC record available at https://lccn.loc.gov/2022003484

Interior design by Janine Agro

Printed in the United States of America

10 9 8 7 6 5 4 3 2 1

*To three masters, to three Sams:*

*Lake,*

*Peckinpah,*

*Shepard.*


*And to three brothers, to three Marianos:*

*Conti,*

*Pettinati,*

*Sánchez.*

# CRUZ

# PART 1
# BROTHERS

# 1.

The last name is a hereditary disease.

Dad's brown eyes and black hair weren't his only gifts to us.

He passed down his demons, too.

It took me a long time to realize that the most important things you inherit can't be packed away in a box.

Or in a coffin.

I had a friend whose father blew his own brains out with a sawed-off. The blood splashed halfway across the wall. It went from red to burgundy, and finally black. My friend didn't know what to do about it. It took him a month to decide to clean the wall. He washed off what he could. The buckshot had buried bits of brain and bone in the pocked cement. My friend scrubbed and scrubbed. He scraped. The brick made it hard for him to know where his dad began and ended. He finally knocked the wall down and put up a new one. Even so, he still goes with his bucket and rag every week to clean it. And he scrubs and scrubs until it's his fingers that bleed on the bricks.

I didn't know what to do with the stuff my old man left me, either. I didn't know how to get rid of it.

Most of it was packed up in boxes for almost fifteen years, piled up in a room in the house that used to be his. A house I've been living in since last summer. Since the first day I moved in, I go to bed every night telling myself that I have to throw his shit out. The answer's always the same: one of these days.

I take out a box filled with my family's rotting remains and set it down next to the other five that are waiting on the sidewalk. A grey dog comes over and sniffs at it. He barks, wanting something from me. Not all skeletons are made of bones. That's what I'd tell him if he could under-stand. He lifts his leg, pisses on the boxes, and trots off wagging his tail.

The last rays of sunlight glow on the dust that floats in the living room and sticks to my sweaty skin. I pull my shirt up from my waist and wipe my face. I let out a long breath, looking at all the work still ahead of me.

In my old man's room, a lamp with more fly shit than wattage shines on boxes stacked together like Tetris blocks. The smell hits me in the face as I enter. I shove a box away from the wall with my leg. A few bugs scatter before bur-rowing deeper into the pile. I stack two boxes and carry them out together. My fingers sink into the cardboard, soggy from the humidity. I manage to set them down with the rest before they come apart completely in my hands.

I should have just burned everything.

On the table is a glass of ice water that turned into warm broth half an hour ago. I pour it on a fern, though it's more in need of a miracle than a watering. I get myself another glass of water and stick my head under the tap before going back to the living room.

It's like there's a mirror between the open doors of the two bedrooms. In mine, boxes that have been collecting dust since I arrived from Buenos Aires, that I'll unpack one of these days. I always think I won't be here much longer, that someone's going to take away the For Sale sign in front of the house.

I drain the glass and get back to work. I take another four boxes out, but the room looks as full as ever. A few doors down, Christmas lights come on and illuminate the front of the house like a shopping mall. In the distance, two more houses blink on and splash color on a girl in a dress and a backpack passing by on her bike. The reflectors in the road shine with the headlights of the Regatta pulling into the garage in front of the house to the left. A guy with a mustache gets out and waves to his neighbor on the other side, who's out watering his garden. He's got all kinds of plants. Red ones. Yellow ones. Purple ones. I should ask him if he has any ideas for my fern. Or just haul it out and leave it with all the other garbage, the cherry on top. They chat for a minute and say goodbye with a smile. The one with the mustache walks by me and waves. He doesn't even say anything about the weather. No "It's a hot one today" or "We sure could do with some rain." I don't even know what his name is.

I'm still surprised by how much is left in the bedroom. Next to the door, there's one solitary box. The last one of the day, I tell myself. This one's heavier than the others. A rotten smell comes out of the hole in the middle and puffs in my face with each step. The box crumbles like a sand castle. I leave it with the others. Three steps later, my foot lands in dog shit. I rub my eyebrows. I fill my lungs. I empty them. The phone rings. Once. Twice. Fuck whoever it is. Three times. It might be my brother. I take off my sneakers and leave them at the door. By the time I make it to the phone, the answering machine has come on: Viviana, my sister-in-law. I pick up.

"Do you know where your brother is?" is her third question.

"I don't know any more than you do."

"Yesterday he called and said he might swing by your place before he came home. He wanted to see you."

"No idea. I haven't talked to Seba in a couple days."

Silence.

"Your niece is asking if we're going to see you before Christmas Eve."

"Tell him to come, Mom." I can hear Violeta's high-pitched voice in the background.

"Come over and we'll order some food."

Why? We're just going to stare at each other, playing a chess game of silences to cover up the questions we're afraid to ask ourselves. Violeta keeps talking.

"Hang on, Lelé," my sister-in-law says. "Okay . . . I'm going to give the phone to this little nag . . ."

"I don't have time. I'm in the middle of something I want to finish."

"What are you doing?"

"Taking out the trash."

Viviana snorts. "Did you open up the back bedroom?" she says. "You're supposed to rest during Christmas vacation, hon. And Seba freed you up from the bar for a couple of days so you could go to Buenos Aires, not sit home and play archaeologist."

More silence. I switch the phone to the other ear. The answering machine has six new messages, even though I was here when they were recorded. They all say pretty much the same thing.

"She called me the other day," Viviana says. "She's worried. She says she calls you and you don't pick up. I told her to come for the holidays because if we leave it up to you . . ."

"Let me take care of my own business."

A bug crawls up my arm and I flick it off. Out the window I see two kids looking at the boxes. One is dragging a cart and eyes my sneakers.

"Tomás . . ." says Viviana.

"What?"

"Stop dicking around and call Alina."

"If I hear from Seba I'll let you know," I say before she can launch into her sermon and I lose my sneakers.

When I get outside, my shoes are still there. The kids are hovering over the boxes. A few photos slip out between the wires of the cart and fall on the red dirt. They're only going to get a few coins for that whole pile of paper.

It's the first time in years my old man's memories have been worth anything.

They see me. One of them taps the other on the shoulder and they stop rummaging.

"Take everything," I say, but they're already hurrying off.

I pick up a photo without looking at it and use it to scrape the shit off my shoe, then throw it back. The wind picks it up and makes it flutter. A couple of grey clouds take bites out of the moon in a pink sky. Night comes early.

I sit on one of the lawn chairs around the living room table. The blinking number six is my only light. It's the closest thing I'll have to Christmas lights this year, and the closest thing to company.

I'll call Alina one of these days.

I look for a beer. In the fridge is a container of mustard, a shriveled head of lettuce, and a rock that used to be bread. I get another glass of water and drink half of it without taking a breath. The fern hasn't perked up. I go over and give it some more water. The garbage truck comes by and picks up the boxes. I feel better.

A shower washes away the sweat and bad mood. For a little while, anyway. Half an hour later, I'm lying in bed sweating like a pig again. I try to watch a movie, but my eyes keep drifting over to the back bedroom and the pile of boxes. I can't even get into *Back to the Future*. I start to nod off. Marty's mom wants to get a look at his package. Boxes. I blink. George McFly finds his balls and beats up the bully. More boxes. I blink. The Doc meets himself. What ever happened to that guy? It must be pretty fucked up to meet yourself. I can't see the boxes anymore.

I open my eyes again. A snake is slithering over Salma Hayek's tits in a rundown whorehouse. Two fifteen on the clock. The same red six blinks on the answering machine. Where's Seba? What did he want to tell me?

I close my eyes. I can't get back to sleep. I turn my back to the door and face my own boxes. What am I going to do with these?

I wish I had to wash a stain off the wall.

The red number six keeps flashing at me. It might never become a seven if I don't do something. I reach out and pick up the cordless phone. I dial the area code for Buenos Aires. The dial tone buzzes. 4957 . . . I take a breath. The sheets stick to my skin. I hang up and exhale.

I don't even know what the hell to do with a few boxes, much less with her and her questions.

One of these days . . . One of these days is another way of saying never.

I stare at a map of water stains on the ceiling. A piece of plaster is hanging from a spiderweb. A mosquito whines in my ear. A car parks outside. I don't recognize the sound of the motor. It's not my brother's truck. And it isn't my sister-in-law's Mondeo, either. It could be a local taxi. A flash of blue light paints the ceiling and tells me it isn't. There's a knock at the door. When I open up, a grey-haired cop takes a step back to let me see the Misiones Police crest on his car. His partner is leaning on the hood with his right hand on his gun.

"Tomás Cruz," says the cop at my door. His nametag says Barrios.

"Whatever that old piece of shit did, I don't care. This time, lock him up and give him life."

"Relax, kid," he says, giving me a smile. "It's not your old man this time."

# 2.

The cruiser heads downtown. Barrios drives and looks at me in the rearview mirror. His smile pinches a scar under his eye, making it disappear in the wrinkles. He looks older when he smiles. And like more of a piece of shit.

"What did he do?" I ask.

"Carried on the family tradition," he says and then turns to his partner, a sergeant whose name badge I didn't manage to read. "You were still sucking on your mom's tit the first time I had a Cruz in the back seat. These two idiots' dad. Good old Samuel. A real tough motherfucker. And smart, too. He could sell gloves to an amputee. For Samuel there are two kinds of people: the ones whose hands he'd shake, and the ones whose hands he'd cut off."

He looks at me again, expecting a comment. When I don't oblige him, he goes on:

"That night we brought him in because he beat up a guy called Leiva who was a witness in a trial against some of

Samuel's friends. We found Leiva lying on the floor of the garage. His wrists were tied up with wire, his left eye was gone, and there were little bits of him everywhere. When he opened his mouth to ask us for help . . . I'll never forget it, kid . . . The three teeth he had left were just hanging from his gums. There was a beer bottle on the floor. The cap was all bitten around the edges and it was covered in little bits of skin. When we asked Samuel about it, all he said was: 'Next time he'll buy himself a bottle opener. Or learn to keep his fucking mouth shut and not act like a *yuru palangana*.'"

The sergeant pushed his fingers against his teeth as if someone was scratching their nails across a blackboard. I've heard worse and better stories about my old man. I stopped caring about them a long time ago. I try to think what part of the family tradition Seba might have carried on. I give up after a minute. There are too many possibilities.

"You should have seen that beer bottle," Barrios says. "All covered in blood. I mean, I've seen my share of shrines to El Gauchito and San La Muerte, but that thing looked like a candle for praying to somebody a hell of a lot worse." Barrios stops talking and crosses himself. "I don't know if El Gaucho or the Reaper always follow through, but Cruz sure as shit does. Leiva knows that better than anybody. I remember wiping his face, but blood kept pouring out of that eye. You can't imagine the puddle he was lying in."

We get stuck at a stoplight. It's the only light on the block.

"How long was he in for?" the sergeant asks.

"Five hours." When the green light floods into the shadows, the cruiser moves forward again. "The next day, Leiva came in all bandaged up like a mummy and said Cruz had acted in self-defense." He laughs. "I guess his memory was as fucked up as his face was. He didn't open his mouth at the trial, and Samuel's buddies went free."

As we move downtown, Posadas becomes brighter. The shirtless people sitting in the doorways of their houses are replaced by people laughing in bars. Everything on the other side of the glass seems far-off and unreal.

"I still remember . . ." Barrios pauses and shakes his head. "Samuel didn't have any ID, but everybody knew him. They said he'd been arrested in a few different provinces. That night I brought him the card to take his prints and said, 'Play it again, Sam.' He looked at me and laughed, and he says, 'Don't worry about the ink' and left all ten prints in Leiva's blood. He raised his boys with those same hands. See? How do you think they'd turn out?"

I've asked myself the same question. I stopped trying to answer it years ago, as soon as I realized it would never lead to anything good.

"Can you just tell me what Seba did?" I say, and I know nothing good will come of that question, either.

"He won a trip to see the place where your old man spent thirteen years. He's going to have a long time to check it out. How long do you think?" he asks his partner.

"Well . . . I'd say five to ten, easy."

"Enough time to know his cell by heart. Maybe he can ask old Samuel for some advice. What do you think, Tomás?"

I don't answer.

"You're right," he continues. "He should have asked *before*. Your old man never would have gone down for something so stupid. He cut a cop's eye out and managed to stay on the outside. His friends did him favors, too."

"He ended up in jail."

"He should have ended up with two in the back and one in the head."

"Well, nobody said life was fair," I say.

"Tell that to your brother," Barrios says, stopping in front of the station.

The sergeant gets out first and opens the door for me.

"Through here," he says.

We walk by a few rooms and down hallways until we reach the officers' desks. A completely blue room. The uniforms. The walls. Even the little Christmas trees have blue garlands. It's stuffy and smells like cigarrettes. Barrios keeps walking and I stay with the kid. Luján, I read on his name badge. That's the name of a famous church. I feel the need to believe in something. In anything.

For a man whose faith is blind, a rosary is a page read in Braille. Luján sits down at his desk. In front of him is a computer screen with an anti-glare protector where I can just make out my brother's information. I can't read what he did.

"Can you tell me anything?"

Barrios peeks his head around a door and waves for Luján to bring me in a little room. Wanted posters billow out in the artificial wind of a rotating fan. Some of them have been there so long they're yellow. Barrios fills out a form and gives it to me. Visitors, I manage to read. My hand shakes as I sign it.

"Do you want to know what he did?" he says.

I nod.

"Look. That didn't fall out of Santa's sleigh."

On top of two tables pushed together are burlap bags spilling over with bricks of marijuana.

"You can see him now," Barrios says and opens the door to the holding cells.

# 3.

The night they took my old man away, the lights on top of five police cruisers painted the world blue. I made it to the front door and saw them herding him down the sidewalk. He had a T-shirt covering his face and his hands cuffed behind his back. Two cuts in his right wrist widened as the blood seeped out.

The shouts had woken me up at dawn. I thought it was my brother and his friends still celebrating that Seba had made the Fourth Division of River Plate; the next day was going to be his debut. As I got up, the shouts became swearing and I realized I was wrong.

As I ran out into the street, my brother caught me and held me tight against him. I managed to pull my face away. The blue lights were spinning. Ten cops made a tunnel that ended at the open back door of a cruiser. The cop closest to us looked at us and laughed. The blood pooled in my father's closed palm and dripped off his fingers. Another cop walked over and pulled the T-shirt off his head. He wanted everyone to see that they'd gotten Samuel Cruz.

I tried to run, to save him. I kicked. I tried to break free. Seba held me tighter. I started to cry. My tears made a dark stain on my brother's shirt.

*Don't take him away. You can't take him away. Tomorrow we were going to see Seba play, Daddy promised me. And this time it's going to be true. This time isn't going to be like the other times.*

I wanted to scream all of that at them, but all I could do was cry as they took him away. Samuel managed to break free long enough to kick the cruiser a few times before five of them shoved him into the back seat. One of the officers picked up his hat, which had fallen into a puddle. Next to the door were three dents. I remember thinking my old man was as strong as a car crash. I tried to see his face. All I found was the back of his head, which was becoming less blue as the cop cars left one by one. I looked at him, waiting for him to turn around and tell us it was all just a mistake. That tomorrow we'd go watch the game. I swore at the cop who stood there laughing. I wanted him to raise his shotgun and shoot me, and then I'd realize the whole thing had been a bad dream. But he just kept laughing and my dad didn't turn around.

His cruiser was the last one to go. The back of my old man's head got smaller and smaller as they drove away. His neck, so thick that even the biggest hands could never have closed around it, looked broken as his head hung toward his chest. Seba hugged me tighter. He stroked my head. His hands were sweaty. A drop fell in my hair, then another. But every time I looked at him, my brother froze the tears in his eyes and said:

"Everything's going to be okay, Tommy. Everything's going to be okay."

He said it over and over, until it was just the two of us sitting alone on the front steps. Right there we promised each other that no matter what happened, we'd be together, that nothing and nobody would ever separate us.

Nothing. Nobody.

**A COUPLE OF HOURS** passed before we went back inside. On my old man's nightstand was the closest thing we would find to a goodbye letter. On top of the glass in a frame that held a picture of the three of us, he'd left his final lines: two straight white rows of blow and a rolled up thousand-austral bill.

My brother grabbed the frame and threw it against the wall. The coke and plaster mixed together in a cloud that settled on the picture, covering us up.

Thirteen years was what they gave my dad. Exactly my age.

And he got off easy. If even a quarter of the things they said about him were true, his rap sheet would have been enough to fill up a whole cell block.

It took me a long time to find out about all that. A really long time. Back then I was just a kid who'd lost his Daddy. By the time *Daddy* became my *old man*, I started to learn the truth, and my *old man* turned into a *son of a bitch*.

When they put him away, I filled up two spiral notebooks with all the days I had to cross out before getting him back. The night I crossed out three hundred fifteen, we got a visit from Alvarenga, my old man's right-hand man. Whenever he came over, he had the same ritual. He unzipped the top pocket if his black leather fanny pack and gave some crumpled bills to my brother. Then he took out a Zippo and lit the hand-rolled cigarette he always had behind his ear. Once he finished it, he'd roll another one and leave.

There were more than a few stories about him and that damn fanny pack. One went that no one had ever seen him without it. A hooker named Maribel even said he left it on when he fucked her. Some people said it was where he kept all the teeth he'd knocked out of people's heads. Everybody else said that was a lie because he would have needed a backpack to fit them all. Another story was that if he unzipped the top pocket, it was to solve a problem for you, but they called the lower one the dead man's pocket. Whenever he unzipped that one, someone wasn't going to see another day.

That same night, my brother had shown up with his head shaved. They'd chosen him to play in the Summer Tournament with the First Division. He was telling Alvarenga about it when I came into the kitchen. My old man's friend grabbed me and rubbed his knuckles in my hair. Then he unzipped the top pocket of his fanny pack and gave me some money. "Get yourself whatever you want, *gurí*," he said. I came back with half the candy aisle from the corner store to celebrate. Alvarenga was standing and patting Seba on the back. My brother was staring at a piece of paper in his hands. When Alvarenga headed for the door, he didn't even see me, almost knocked me over. I stumbled backwards. The fanny pack was level with my eyes. The bottom pocket hung open in a smile. He zipped it up and grabbed a chocolate bar from me, sticking a new cigarette behind his ear.

My brother was still starting at the wrinkled piece of paper between his fingers. Three names and addresses were scribbled on it.

"What's that?"

The first inheritance our old man had left us, I'd find out later. My brother folded the slip of paper and put it in his shirt pocket.

"A couple of things I have to take care of. Don't worry about it."

The day I crossed out three hundred thirty, Seba crossed out the first name on the list. Six days later, the second one.

One night, not long after that, the phone rang. It was the soccer club. My brother hadn't shown up, and the bus needed to leave for Mar del Plata.

"I don't know where he is."

"Tell him if he doesn't show up, don't bother coming back."

I fell asleep waiting for him, looking at his new cleats sticking out of his half-packed gym bag.

The front door slamming woke me up at three in the morning. His bed, next to mine, was still empty. I heard him grunt and go into the bathroom. There were dark droplets shining on the wood of the door. As I peeked my head around, I could see him in the mirror wiping blood from a cut in his eyebrow. His lip was split. He threw something into the sink, which swung heavily from side to side. He sat down on the toilet and started to cry. Someone knocked at the front door. I saw Alvarenga's car and ran to hide. Seba went out shirtless to talk to him.

"Your old man didn't exactly leave you guys a debt," Alvarenga said with a short laugh. "Not in money, anyway. And these people . . ."

I stopped listening. I went into the bathroom. The T-shirt on the floor was leaving a puddle that crawled along the grout between the tiles to create a cage of blood on the floor. The piece of paper was crumpled up in the trash can. In the sink was a 9mm that had left scratch marks in the ceramic.

And the cage kept growing.

The sound of the door slamming sent me running back into the bedroom. I caught a glimpse of Seba leaning against the wall with another slip of paper in his hands.

As he cleaned himself up in the bathroom, I looked at

his gym bag again. He'd hung up his brand-new cleats. I opened a drawer, took out my notebooks, and threw them in the trash.

My brother turned off the light. I heard him stop in the doorway to look at me. I pretended to be asleep.

I didn't know what to say.

There was nothing I could say.

He didn't get into his bed that night.

My brother went into my old man's room and made it his own, and I realized that sooner or later, he was going to end up in the same places our father did.

# 4.

My brother is waiting in the middle of the room, hand-cuffed to a painted metal table.

He doesn't look at me. Not even when I walk over and sit down in front of him. The chair rocks on the uneven floor. With the index finger of his free hand, Seba picks at the O of a RATI PUTO, fuck the police, gouged into the paint on the table until he makes it a hole.

Since the night he locked himself in our old man's room, my brother has been living as two people. One, the family man, the father, the husband, the brother; and the other, the businessman, who would disappear and come back with a bag of money or a scar. The part that made me remember ignorance is bliss.

"They gave me my old number back," Seba says, nodding at the number 3 above the cell's open door.

In his first soccer club, way before he'd ended up in River, they used to play Seba as a fullback. He didn't like it one bit. He scored so many goals the coach had no option but to give Seba a chance to play forward. And that's where he'd won the number 11.

"If I have to be honest, I liked it better when you played defense. Any klutz can play forward. To be a defender, you need personality. You were someone else on the field. You wouldn't let anyone pass you. Especially because you knew one-armed Almada was the goalie."

His hair is stuck to his muddy face. His T-shirt, which used to be white, is the color of a rushing river. My brother looks like something that floated to the surface after a flash flood.

"Almada . . . I had forgotten about that son of a bitch. He was playing for Colegiales a while back. He sucks even more now that he's older. But at least he is still playing."

He lowers his head, hits the table twice. Chips of varnish fall off.

"I fucked up, Tommy," he says. "I fucked up."

That's how the two parts start to come together and let me see what's on the other side.

"I was good at soccer. The day I hung up my cleats was one of the worst days of my life. I see guys who used to play with me in the pro leagues now. Here or over in Europe, kicking ass. Making a fortune. Doing what they love. And it kills me not knowing where I would have ended up, never finding out how good I was."

He tugs at his left hand. The cuffs stop his hand with a

jerk and cut into his wrist. He moves his right hand over and scratches his arm. The dried mud looks like scales on his skin and a few chunks flake off onto the table.

"And this," he says, pointing at the cuffs, "I didn't choose this. I just happened to be good at this, too. And sooner or later, if you're good at something, you end up liking it, needing it.

"When everything went to shit in Buenos Aires, I felt worse than the day I stopped playing soccer. Even though I'd already done what I had to. I felt like shit because I was already too old to go back to soccer. But in this business . . . maybe I could make a comeback there. I didn't want to keep wondering what the hell happened. And it was the right call."

That's one way to put it. We'd gotten some money out of selling the house in Buenos Aires. My brother used it to open the bar he owned and I worked in. It was great, we made money hand over fist even through there were never more than ten people in there drinking. There was more movement on the deposit slips than at the tables, but the register was always full. That's where my two years studying accounting and Alvarenga's tricks for laundering money came in handy. My brother's life was looking up. He switched out his rusty Taurus for a Ford Ranger, and his studio apartment for a three-bedroom house with a front yard. Violeta was enrolled at a private school.

"You know what, Tommy? I learned two things today," he says. "One, that I'm no good at this. And two, that Río de la Plata isn't the widest river in the world. The widest river in the world is the one you have to cross in a boat loaded with fifty kilos of weed." He closes his eyes. He takes a deep breath and exhales through his nose. "It was so fast. They came out of nowhere . . ."

He shakes his head, opens his eyes. He looks me in the eye for a moment.

I don't say anything.

There's nothing to say.

I can hear the sound of a fan overhead. Laughter too, I think. Maybe. When I listen closely, I can't hear it. Seba scratches at his arm a little more.

"The DA's sending me straight to jail. He says I'm a flight risk, or that I could intimidate witnesses. Bullshit. The truth is they're putting me away for possession of a last name." His smile cracks the muddy wrinkles around his mouth. "But don't worry. My lawyer said out of the fifty keys, they only logged twenty. And by the time they finish divvying it up in here, they'll be locking me up for a few joints. I'll get three years, tops."

"Three years . . ."

My brother stretches. With his free hand, he grabs my forearm and says again:

"Don't worry, everything's going to be fine. If that old fuck could take thirteen years, three's nothing." His fingers pinch my skin. He looks me dead in the eyes. "I have to ask you a favor."

His face crumples in a grimace and he shows me the palm of his cuffed hand.

"I need you to take care of them for me," he says.

"Of course." I put my hand on top of his.

He lowers his eyes. He takes a deep breath, but it's not in relief. It's more like he's psyching himself up for something.

"What is it, Seba? Tell me."

"I didn't want to do this job. It didn't sound right. But I'd fucked up before, Tommy. They didn't give me much choice: they said that whatever happened, they'd give me two ounces. I just had to choose of what. Two ounces of cash for me, or two ounces of lead for my wife and daughter . . ."

His voice falters. He pulls his lips in between his teeth, the wrinkles on his forehead come together in a web, and dried mud falls on the table. He pulls at his left hand, forgetting about the cuffs. He takes his right hand off my arm and tries to cover his face, but one hand isn't enough.

"Seba . . . tell me."

"They need someone to finish the job. I need you to take care of my family. Can I count on you?"

Seba's fingers dig into my arm again. The dirt melts and becomes slippery with our sweat.

"Tommy, can I trust you?"

I think about all the promises that must have been made across this table. To stay together or move on. And all the shit in between. A whole lot of shit, because the hardest promises to keep are the ones you make to desperate people.

When people are desperate, they ask you to do the impossible.

"Of course, brother. Of course."

He lets me go, and I can see his marks of his fingers printed in mud on my arm. I want to, but I can't bring myself to tell him everything's going to be okay. I hear banging overhead. The metal door clangs against the wall and Barrios comes down the stairs. My brother leans in as close as he can and whispers to me:

"Alvarenga will call you tomorrow." He gives me half a hug.

That's what's left of him. Half a hug and a promise that sounds an awful lot like a debt. As I climb the stairs, I think about the door to my old man's room opening up again.

WHEN I GET HOME, there's a blinking red number seven waiting for me. I sit down in a lawn chair. Each blink separates my body from the darkness. I stand up and hit play.

"Hi, Tom. It's Alina. I wanted to let you know . . ."

"Message erased. Next mess . . . Message erased."

And on through all seven, until there's nothing left but shadows and one truth. The past is the one thing that nobody can take away from you, no matter what you owe them.

# 5.

"The first time I saw your brother," says my sister-in-law, "he was sitting at a bar picking the label off a bottle of beer. He just sat there like that for half an hour. Didn't even take a drink."

Cigarette smoke comes out of Viviana's silhouette against the window. The amber light filters in through the slats of the shade, and the rotating fan cools the sweat on my back, then rustles the dry leaves of the fern. The only thing deader than that plant is the phone. A song by *NSYNC is playing in my room. My niece sings along. She printed out the lyrics she found online on the blank side of my Anatomy I notes, a memento of the two years I'd tried to become a doctor before thinking maybe accounting was more my thing. My niece is making better use of those notes than I ever did. Her voice is indifferent.

Viviana stubs out her half-smoked cigarette and starts playing with the lighter, spinning it between her fingers.

We're sitting in the lawn chairs, staring at the wall as if we were looking at the ocean. There are just a few nails here and there.

"My mom worked as a waitress for five years," Viviana goes on. "She said that people who ordered something and didn't drink it had either just fucked up big time or were getting ready to. All I saw was a guy who needed a smile. When he looked over at me for the third time, I gave him one, and he gave me one back." Her face is lit by a red glare, then disappears behind the smoke of a new cigarette. "Since Seba didn't get up, I made the first move. I sat down next to him and asked him if he was waiting for someone. He nodded. But before I could leave, he stopped me. He asked if I knew anything about horse racing. I said I had no idea. And he says, 'The guy I'm waiting for doesn't know anything about it either, but he likes to bet. A lot.' And he nods toward this guy sitting at a table reading a newspaper. Another guy gets up and walks over to give him a little piece of paper and an envelope, and he puts it in his pocket really quick. 'So now I'm in a tough spot,' he says. 'The only thing this Bayerque guy likes more than gambling is painting. And he's actually good at that. I don't know shit about art. But my brother told me it's not about understanding it, it's about feeling it.'"

She looks up at me and takes a drag on her cigarette. She blows out the smoke, and the fan hits it, dissolving the cloud.

"So he bought me a beer and while the guy with the paper kept taking bets and envelopes, Seba told me stuff about this guy Bayerque. That he'd been to his workshop and the guy was finishing up a painting of a man and a dog walking across a beach toward a house. 'They were totally alone,' your brother said. 'It could have been sad. But what I liked was that the waves washed away their footprints. I've never been to the ocean, but I could feel what it was like for them there, and because they didn't leave any footprints, they had no past. It was just that moment.'"

She takes one last drag on the cigarrette and stubs it out in the ashtray. There are already seven half-smoked cigarettes there, bent like the legs of a crab made of ash.

"I remember wondering what was going on in your brother's head that he spent so much time thinking about that damn painting to avoid it. I wanted to give him a good answer, but all that came out was: 'I'd like to see his paintings.' 'You better hurry up before they're all taken out of the country,' he said. 'Or he loses them all.' He told me that morning his boss had called him in. When he got into the office he saw the painting of the beach. It had been appraised at fifty thousand dollars. Bayerque had ended up selling it for five thousand pesos. But he still owed thirty. And that's where Seba came in. 'The rules are simple,' he said. 'For fifty thousand or more, I'd have to break his leg. For thirty, an arm.'"

She drums her fingers on the table. It's the first time I've seen her without nail polish.

"So there was your brother. Trying to figure out what to

do. I should have been scared, but Seba sounded so guilty, almost like it was his arm that was going to get broken. He asked me what I would do. 'Get a new job,' I said. He laughed. Well, snorted like he does. He wanted to know what a girl like me was doing there at that time of day. I told him I was at a crossroads, too. I liked that word. Your brother always came up with some kind of crazy word. I told him I was there to end a relationship, as if there was anything to end. I was his girlfriend, but I was the only woman for miles he wasn't sleeping with. 'I guess that means I won't be seeing him anymore,' I said. 'What about you?' I asked him that just as a guy walked in. Seba took one of the beer labels that was already dry and wrote down his name and number. 'I'm going to buy you a drink.' And he gave me his number with a smile. When I left, he was putting his hand on the shoulder of the guy who'd just come in.

"Three days later, I called him and we planned to meet up at the same bar. I was waiting for him when I saw Bayerque come in. His right arm was in a cast, and he was giving an envelope to the guy with the newspaper. Your brother showed up and didn't even bother looking at him. He came over to me and took my arm like a gentleman. 'Let's go, my lady,' he said. He took me to a really nice place for dinner. Candles, hors d'oeuvres, first course, second course, the whole shebang. But his head was somewhere else. I kept thinking about that cast until I finally asked him about it over dessert. He looked at me really serious and he said, 'If it doesn't hurt, they don't learn.' And then he had a spoonful of the dessert. 'You've got to try this.'" She coughs out a laugh. "That was the only time I heard about what he did. Until now."

She opens up her pack of cigarettes and realizes it's empty. I peel myself off the lawn chair and stand up to get a glass of water. The phone still hasn't rung. I pick it up. There's a dial tone. I lean against the door frame of my old man's room. Lelé smiles at me. Her nails are painted, even though Viviana almost never lets her do that.

"I only got up the courage once to ask him what he really did, and he asked me why I wanted to know. 'To know who I'm sharing my bed with,' I said. 'With a good man. The rest of the day, I do what I have to. Nothing that's going to make the world a better place. Or a worse place.' We never talked about it again. He would just clam up. And I thought maybe that was best. His way of dealing with what happened. Sometimes he'd show up hurt or drunk. But he kept it to himself. Whenever he came into our life, he always gave us his best. I'd watch the two of them play. I saw how he made Lelé smile. And that was enough for me. A bad person couldn't show that kind of love."

Her neck is shiny with sweat, and her hair sticks to it. The fan blows at wisps of her hair coming out of a pony tail that looks like it's about to fall down completely.

"He told me you were going to take care of everything," she says.

I nod. We look at each other for a moment. Long enough

to trust each other. Long enough not to stop trusting each other.

I think about my old man's room and my room with that pile of boxes waiting there. Then the dried out fern. 'Everything' is a word that's too big for me.

"Aren't you going to have a Christmas tree, Uncle Tommy?"

Lelé is next to me. She has a plaid barrette, and her blond hair looks white in the rays of sunlight falling on her head.

"I left it in Buenos Aires," I tell her.

The last time there was a Christmas tree in this house, Samuel had pulled up a bush from the neighbor's yard. My brother asked if we could put something on it to decorate it. My old man came back with some red wires he'd torn out of the wall and put them up like garlands. "Do you guys want some snow?" We said yes. He took the cigarrette out of his mouth and tapped it twice on top of the bush. "Is that good or do you want more?"

"But there'll be presents, right?"

"Of course, sweetie."

"Are you clearing out space, Uncle Tommy?" she says, looking at my old man's room.

"Something like that."

"Is Alina going to come live with you?"

My sister-in-law looks at her daughter as if to say the only thing bigger than her mouth is her heart. My niece waits for an answer. She doesn't look away.

"Maybe."

"Get your stuff together," Viviana tells her, "it's time to go." She waits until Lelé goes into my room. "I promised her we'd go see the Nativity scene. A few of her school friends are going to go with their parents. She's asking if Daddy's coming with us. I said he was still traveling. I still don't know how to tell her."

"You'll find a way."

Lelé comes over and gives me a kiss. She goes out first and stands next to the door of the Mondeo. Across the street, a white Isuzu truck starts up and the horn beeps twice. A hand waves at us and disappears behind the tinted window.

"Who was that, Mom?"

My sister-in-law comes over to me and says, "He was at the door of my house today. What the hell is going on? What are we going to do, Tomás?"

"I'll take care of it," I tell her, watching the white Isuzu disappear around the corner. Once it's gone, my sister-in-law gets in her car and drives off in the opposite direction.

I close the door behind me, a million questions exploding in my head, one after the other. *If you you don't want to think, you have to act* was painted on a wall in the neighborhood when I was a kid. So while I wait, I go back into my old man's room.

I take out a box to keep from thinking about how my brother's doing.

Two, to keep from going crazy trying to imagine why

Alvarenga hasn't called and what the hell I'm going to have to do.

Three, to keep from thinking about what Alina wants.

Four, five, ten boxes. But the truth is they could clear cut the Amazon and make it into boxes, but it still wouldn't be enough to keep my mind off all the shit I don't want to think about.

Samuel's room is half empty. As I pick up a box, an image comes into view. On the wall, I see where we used to measure how tall we were. Our heights are mixed in with phone numbers and names scrawled on the paint. I remember him shutting himself up in there, awake all night. The sound of his sniffling. When I was little, I thought my old man always had a cold. It took me a few years to realize he was doing coke constantly. I think about all the times I knocked on his door with a cup of tea with lemon and honey so he'd feel better.

I see a few cigarrette burns on the carpet. The nights he left the door open, it was always the same scene. Him waiting for a phone call. Emptying bottles. Filling ashtrays. A cigarrette forgotten between the fingers of his right hand, leaving him a wedding band of burns.

He'd given his lifelong vows to all that.

At least he'd sworn loyalty to something.

I look at the empty living room. The yellow lawn chairs next to an oak table, the nails waiting for paintings, photos, mirrors. Anything. A plant that won't quite die. The framework for a life I never built. The boxes in my bedroom are pieces I don't know how to fit together. I swear loyalty to that. To leaving things. To waiting for stuff to happen.

I spend the next hour looking from the street to the phone and back again. I think again about what Alina wanted to tell me.

A knock at the door makes me jump in my lawn chair. I go over and look out the bedroom window. The white Isuzu isn't there. There aren't any other cars, either. I let out my breath when I see who it is. I open the door. Now I know what she wanted to tell me.

White tank top and jean shorts. Her brown hair looks reddish when I turn on the living room light.

"Hi, Tom," says Alina, before giving me a kiss and coming inside.

# 6.

A while ago, Alina told me there are two types of people. People who say "I love you" and people who say "Me, too."

"You're not the first kind," she said.

Before Alina, my relationships, if you could call them that, were a couple of dates, a lot of beer or liquor together but very few breakfasts, and when it was time to make it official, I'd play dumb until they finally got sick of it. A "Me, too" can't give something you don't give them first.

Then Alina showed up. There was something in the way she looked at me with those green eyes that made me feel calm. I didn't want to run away anymore. I stopped being me, to become us. And I understood how important that word was.

I understood that "us" is the word.

The problem with getting what you want is being afraid to lose it. Thinking about that drove me crazy. I spent a year like that. Two. Living with her but wanting to run, to go back to being just me. And on the other hand, wanting to be a family. Now there's a word I didn't believe in.

My brother would drop Lelé off for us to take care of her, and I could see how Alina looked at my niece. I saw what she wanted, something I couldn't give her. I'd drop off the map for a couple of weeks. Instead of tearing me a new one, she'd be there waiting for me with open arms. Alina had faith in the things that are the hardest to believe in. She had faith in me. In us.

Until my brother said: "I'm getting out of here, Tommy." "Me, too," I said. I didn't ask him where we were going. When I told her, she cried, she yelled at me, but in the end she gave me one last kiss and told me we'd find a way.

We lied to ourselves, doing the long-distance thing for a few months. Then I couldn't take it anymore. I disappeared just like I used to. The only way she heard my voice was in the recording on the answering machine telling her to leave a message. She filled a whole cassette. Then she stopped calling. She started dating another guy. I was with a few girls I can barely remember.

Eventually we realized that distance kills everything except what's really worth it. I called her. I told her the truth. I stopped being a "Me, too." She turned up at my house. I remember the reunion. We went into the bedroom and she started crying when she came. She'd given me a potted fern to bring a little life into the house, to make it a home. A couple of visits later, the two of us knew things weren't going anywhere. We were making up more than we were making love. Three months ago, she told me she needed to know where we were going from here. I just lay there in silence, my eyes on the closed door of my old man's room.

"What are you looking at? What's in that room?" she asked, letting out the question that had been stuck in her throat since the first time she came here.

"The stuff that doesn't belong in this house," I said.

There was silence until she said: "Then I should go sleep in there."

She got up and went to open the door. I tried to stop her, say something to her, but I couldn't. She grabbed the keys to my car. "Go pick it up at the bus station," she said, before starting up the Peugeot 206 and disappearing.

That was the last time I'd seen her.

NOW, ALINA'S STANDING RIGHT in front of me.

"Thanks for picking me up," she says. She looks at the zero on the answering machine. "You don't even listen to your messages anymore?"

"What are you doing here?"

"I was headed to Iguazu Falls and I thought, why not visit Tom while I'm here."

She puts her purse down on the table and opens it. She digs around until she finds a hair tie. Alina clicks her tongue, remembering there are no mirrors in the house. She goes over to the window and uses her reflection to pull her hair back.

"Do you want some coffee?" I ask. "Water?"

She finishes with her hair. She narrows her eyes when she sees that the door to my old man's room is open. I close it. She starts to say something but ends up just looking around the living room.

"No mirrors, no pictures. There's not even a calendar. With this passion for minimalist decoration, someone might think you're a simple man."

"I'm going to make myself a coffee. Do you want one?"

"There you go. I haven't even been here five minutes and you're already looking for a way to escape."

"You traveled six hundred miles to have a fight?"

I fill up the kettle and put it on the stove. The only coffee cup is in the sink, dirty. Two flies come buzzing out before the water from the tap hits them.

"Do you want some or not?" I say when I'm back in the living room.

"I want you to sit down so we can talk."

"This isn't the best time."

"Well, when is the best time? When I call you and you don't pick up? When you get the nerve to call me, and five minutes later you're back to silence? I think this is the best time." She nods her head toward the door of my old man's room. "Looks like you've been getting rid of some of the old junk you had kicking around, so why don't you tell me where that leaves me?"

When she sits down on one of the lawn chairs, her shorts creep up her legs.

"I spend half my nights thinking what an asshole you are and telling myself I'm an idiot to keep trying to make it work with you." A truck passes outside. I can't see what color it is, much less the model. "The other half, I convince myself to do crazy shit like this, to come and stay with you." She pauses to take a breath. "We can't keep being messages on answering machines."

She brings her knees up against her chest. Her feet are covered in red dust, and white lines peek out from under the straps of her flip-flops.

"What are you thinking?" she says. Her favorite question.

About why the hell Alvarenga hasn't called.

"That you're right," I say.

"So, what then?"

A truck goes by again. White. It could be the Isuzu. I go over to the window and raise the blind a little more.

"This seriously isn't a good time, Alina."

"What's wrong?"

I don't answer.

"We're hitting rock bottom here, Tom." She says it sadly. She takes off her anger like a dress. "I call you and you call me back three days later if I'm lucky. If I stop calling you, then you're the one calling me. You like to stretch things out as far as they'll go. I just can't take it anymore." She grabs her ponytail and pulls it across her mouth. "I always wanted things to be different. That's why I kept trying. I'm tired as hell, but here I am to give it one last try. Because if I sit around waiting for you to do it, we're dead."

She stretches out her feet, and her flip-flips dangle from her toes. Her legs are tanned. I want to touch them. I want her to wrap them around me and not have to answer any more questions. I scratch my neck. I look at the phone.

"What's wrong with you? Are you expecting a call?"

"Something like that."

"Oh . . . sorry. I didn't know I was interrupting. I'm such an idiot." She looks at the ceiling. "What's her name?"

"Don't be stupid."

I realize the water's been boiling for a few minutes, go into the kitchen to turn off the burner. The tiles and windowpanes are steamy. The Christmas lights on the other side of the glass twinkle and grow, melting together like colored stars.

"Tomorrow is our three-and-a-half-year anniversary," Alina says when I come back. "Even if you say every month that it's the last one we'll be together. I'm sick of wondering whether it's because you don't love me or because you're scared of God knows what." I go over to put my arms around her, but she moves away. "I want us to be good. But I need to know what it is you want, and for you to make a decision."

The sound of a car engine approaches slowly. The beams

of the headlights cut across the ground. Yes. It's the white Isuzu. It honks. Suddenly, I realize Alina is still talking.

"Are you listening to me? Are you high?"

The phone rings and I rush over to answer it.

"Tomás?"

"Yeah."

"What's up, *gurí*? It's Alvarenga. Come over to the Tanimbu. Our bar's full of cops." His voice moves away from the phone and talks to someone else. "Is she here? Tell her to come in. Sorry, kid. I'm here. Just come. I'll be waiting." And he hangs up.

"Can you tell me what's going on?" Alina insists. "Come on, Tomás. Talk to me."

"My brother asked me to go see someone."

She blinks twice. Her eyebrows go up. I wonder what she's been able to read on my face.

"What did he do?"

"I don't know. I don't know anything." I look through the slats of the blinds. The white Isuzu is parked half a block away. I grab the keys to the house and the car. "Come on."

"Where are we going? We're having a conversation here."

"I have to go see this guy. Right now."

"I'm tired and all grimy. Go ahead and I'll wait for you. I'll take a shower and see if I can calm down a little, and we can talk when you get back."

"I want you to come with me," I say, taking her hand.

"You're acting weird."

"I think that's a good thing."

She gives me a smile that fades away when she bites her lip.

"Let me at least have a quick shower."

"Don't worry. You're going to be the prettiest girl in the place just the way you are."

"The prettiest girl in the place . . ." she says, laughing. "What kind of shithole are you taking me to?" She grabs her purse and hangs it from her shoulder. "Let's get going, then. I need a cold beer."

"Me, too," I say, and immediately kick myself for it.

We get into the 206 and drive off. In the rearview, the white Isuzu makes a U-turn and starts to follow us. One block. Another. It flashes its lights at me and then turns.

I don't know Morse code, but I'm sure they were saying, "See you later."

# 7.

The neon lights of the riverside bars spill color on the groups of people drinking at the tables outside. Farther down is the lookout point, where people on beach blankets drink their last *tereré* before switching over to something a little stronger. I can see a string of cars moving slowly in the rearview.

Alina purses her lips from side to side. She changes the station, tango, cumbia, until she finds a song I think is by Dave Matthews. She taps her foot. I don't know if she's following the rhythm or is just nervous.

"Are we almost there?" she says. "I have to go to the bathroom."

"We're just about there."

The Paraná River peeks out around the curve. Rather than meeting its own reflection, the city seems to sink into the water. I look in the rearview again. Once I'm sure we aren't being followed, I turn south. Alina doesn't even bother talking. She rests her head against the door again and squeezes her hands between her knees. She just accepts the situation. She's used to it.

The streets go from having names to numbers. The asphalt turns to dirt, and the sidewalks, to grass. Mosquitoes buzz around the few streetlights that work. On the other side of the creeping vines, kids play in a pool. A couple of girls dance in flip-flops in the door of a makeshift bar in someone's garage. On top of a fruit crate, a baby breastfeeds while its mother drinks a liter bottle of beer.

"Tell me this isn't it," Alina says.

"It's on the next block."

"Good. I really need to pee."

My brother's bar doesn't hold a candle to the ones on the Riverside, but at least it's a place where you can sit and have a beer, and the only protection you might need can be purchased from the condom vending machine in the bathroom. On the other hand, when I park in front of the Tanimbu, the protection I want is more along the lines of a bullet-proof vest. The front of the building is brick and cement with different-colored stains. One of the two windows is covered with corrugated aluminum and posters of people who've gone missing, many of them seen for the last time in this very bar.

Five people sitting at the table next to the door look up at us. Their eyes shine. I think I know the only woman sitting there. One of the guys, too. There's one I can't see behind a wall of Quilmes bottles. He pushes them aside like a curtain. White wife-beater, 300 pounds, 50 of which are in his red nose covered in burst veins. The Dart Galarza. Sometimes he does jobs for my brother—when he isn't drunk. Galarza does less work than a politician. Nobody thinks twice about buying him a drink. That way you're sure that when his mind finally snaps, he won't stab you with the gaucho knife he carries in his belt. The other four put their heads down and carry on talking, but Galarza's giving me the evil eye. Just me. He doesn't even look at Alina. Everybody else looks at her, though. I'm sure they think ET's more likely to walk in there than a girl like her.

"What kind of mess did your brother get himself into?" she asks.

I take her hand and lead her to the bar at the back. There are high stools with torn pleather and what's left of the stuffing peeking out. The bartender's over six feet. He's wearing a white apron covered in red stains, like a butcher. He hasn't got a shirt on under it, and his skin is covered in greenish tattoos, souvenirs from time on the inside.

"I'll just hold it," Alina says and laughs nervously, moving her legs.

"Hey, man," I say to the bartender, who doesn't take his eyes off *Jingle All the Way* on the TV set into the wall. He needs another "Hey, man" to react. He stares at Alina as if I wasn't there.

"What can I get for such a beautiful lady?"

"We're looking for Alvarenga," I say.

Schwarzenegger pours whiskey into a dog dish. The bartender laughs.

"I had a dog just like that. He was really loyal. One time a doberman came in, and . . ."

"It's a reindeer," Alina says. The guy blinks in confusion.

"Alvarenga," I repeat. "Have you seen him?"

The bartender puts a toothpick in his mouth and leans both arms on the bar. He has a gun tattooed on one, and on the other, the Virgin of Luján. They look like they were drawn by a five-year-old.

"And who the hell are you?"

"Cruz."

Someone coughs at the table next to the door. One guy who's sitting down doesn't take his eyes off Alina's ass, and when he licks his lips he shows off the three teeth he's got left. She pulls at her shorts, and ends up standing in front of me to hide.

"Are you Cruz's kid?" asks the bartender, pointing his toothpick at me.

"Tomás Cruz," Alina says. "He's looking for Alvarenga. Should I write it down for you?"

"Cruz," he repeats and walks over to use the rotary phone at the other end of the bar.

"This guy's a real detective." Alina puts her face next to my ear, resting her head on my shoulder. If she's afraid, she's not showing it. We've gotten close before, but this is the first time in a long time that I've felt like we were together.

The bartender hangs up and comes back over to us.

"He says to wait." He points at a metal door next to the bathrooms at the back of the bar. "You want something to drink?" We haven't finished telling him no before he's back to watching the movie.

In a mirror covered in mold and damp, I see Galarza eyeing us as we sit down on a couple of plastic chairs. The table's covered in peanut shells and cigarrette butts. Alina sits with her back to everyone, facing the bathrooms. There's so little light that her reddish-brown hair looks black. Three cockroaches scuttle down the wall, and a few feet farther down disappear under the door of one of the two bathrooms.

"What the hell are we doing here, Tom?"

"A favor for my brother."

She opens and closes her mouth, like she's rewinding her words and putting them away. She reaches across the table and takes my hand.

"I'm sorry," I say.

"You're not a Cruz," says Galarza, raising his voice. "There's two things this little pussy doesn't deserve. That piece of ass there and that last name."

I squeeze my hands into fists. I forget I'm holding her hands, which slip away.

"Don't worry about it," Alina says quietly. "Don't listen to him."

The bartender kills a cockroach crawling across the TV screen with a snap of his bar towel. Two legs stay stuck to the screen. Alvarenga, what the fuck are you doing?

"What are you talking about?" asks one of the other guys at the table. "You drunk already, Galarza?"

"That there is the son of the great Cruz."

"What Cruz?" says the other kid, whose face is covered in pockmarks.

"What do you mean, what Cruz? Samuel Cruz." He looks at the woman. "Betti, didn't you teach your kids history?"

The woman and the other man just nod in agreement. The way you do with crazy people. With drunk people. I don't know. I also don't know which story Galarza's going to tell. What I do know is who they are. Betti. Ten kids, no husband. She makes her living on small-time contraband, watches and clothes, and when money's tight she loads up bricks of weed right along with her kids. These two must be her oldest. The other guy is Trota. He worked with my brother until his wife told him she needed to be with someone who had an honest job. He ended up working for a wood pulp company that pollutes rivers and levels forests. "I had to choose which cancer I wanted," he'd said.

"Old Cruz was an animal. Not like this little bitch," says Galarza. "I had the honor of helping him out one time. You remember that, Trota?" He elbows him, and Trota just empties his glass. A burp inflates his cheeks. "The Di Pietros. You know that name?" The two kids nod. "Well, that Cruz worked for old man Di Pietro, the father of the guy you all work for. That was Anibal Senior. So the thing is Anibal Junior had been a fucking mess since he was a kid. You guys think he chases tail now, but he used to be a real snake. He used to go out with a *cate* from his neighborhood, but then he went crazy over this *bugre* bitch from Puerto Piray. So little Anibal was always going back and forth to see this girl. One time we were sitting around with Samuel getting shitty at Tote's, and Anibal Senior shows up. He says hey to both of us and says he's got a job for us. Well, he said it to Cruz, but I was with him. I used to roll with them, you know. So he takes Samuel to the back and says, 'They took my kid.'"

With a shaky hand, one of Betti's kids examines the bottles on the table like he's picking over the dead on a battlefield, and finally finds one with a little swill left at the bottom.

"Are you listening to me?" Pockface nods. "So Cruz comes back over and says we got a job. He tells me to stay there in case Alvarenga shows up. He was in Paraguay. So I see him again two days later. And he says, 'I need your house. I can't do it at mine 'cause my kids are there.' I was on my own then because Mirta left me. You remember Mirta, Trota? She had those eyes, remember? They always shined."

"She had a fucking glass eye, man."

"She was still pretty."

Alina looks at me. It's the closest she's ever come to being introduced to my old man. Maybe she understands now why

I never told her anything. Maybe she understands what I'm afraid of. Maybe she's just trying to hear the movie.

"Anyway . . . we go back to my place. Cruz opens the trunk of his Fairlane and pulls out a guy trussed up like a pig. We take him to the garage and Cruz ties him to a chair. 'I got this,' I tell him. But he says, 'No, Galarza. You got a fucking arm on you and you'll kill the guy.' Then he goes out to the car and comes back with a tackle box. Man, the times we stayed up all night fishing. He opens up the box and there are more levels in there than an apartment building in Buenos Aires. 'You stay here and turn up the music.' I put on some *chamamé* as high as that shit'll go, and even so I could hear the screams in a couple of minutes. I don't know who that motherfucker worked for. He screamed and screamed but he didn't say a goddamn thing. I went in to check it out, and it was a real work of art. You seen all those pussies nowadays with rings hanging off them everywhere?"

"Piercings," says Pockface, grabbing one in his own eyebrow.

"Yeah, that shit. Well, Cruz put that guy ahead of his time. Motherfucker was covered in fishhooks."

"Ah, shut up, Galarza. You're so full of shit," says the other guy at the table.

Galarza slaps him on the back of his head. Alina jumps in her chair and then goes back to chewing on her fingernails. She's fanning at her hair stuck to her neck. Come the fuck on, Alvarenga.

"I'm not fucking with you. In his eyebrows, in his chest, in his arms. You shoulda seen it. And the guy didn't talk."

"Bullshit, Dardo, you are such a *yapú*."

"Tell them, Betti." She nods and raises her hand to order another beer. There's no waiter, and the bartender is still watching the movie. "Since he didn't have any luck with the fishhooks, he took another look in the tackle box. 'Turn it up,' he says. So I put on Palito Ortega. Double torture. And Cruz rolled up his sleeves and got creative. 'You're looking a little fat,' he says to the guy. 'I'm going to take off some of that extra weight. First you can get off your chest the address where they've got the Di Pietro kid, and then I'll help you with a couple of pounds. But first I'll fatten you up a little. Let's see how much you can take,' he says. Medieval weight-lifting, he said it was called. He grabbed some fishing line and tied on a few sinkers. Then he started hanging them on the hooks he'd put in the guy's face. You should have seen how his skin stretched out. He started with one he'd put in his cheek, one of those deals with three hooks, he'd stuck two of those in his face. Boom. Sinker. Boom. Sinker. His cheeks started to pull down like a goddamn bulldog."

Alina looks at me, serious. She's not disgusted. For the first time, it's as if the clouds are lifting away from my past and she can see what's behind them. She reaches out and strokes my arm.

"Boom. Sinker," Galarza goes on, hitting the table with every 'boom.' Two bottles of beer fall on the floor. No one says anything. "Boom. Sinker. Until his skin just gives and all that's left are rolled-up shreds. Fucker looked like pulled pork. It's a good thing I got a strong stomach. And that was it. The guy told him everything. He and Alvarenga went over to check the place out. They had the Di Pietro kid way out in East Bumfuck. So they went back the next day with a couple of automatics. I asked them for a piece and they said, 'No, Galarza, you're too crazy. Stay here and keep decorating this asshole.'" Trota shakes his head. "And they left. There were like seven guys in the house where they had Anibal Junior. But those two were like an army. If we'd had them in the Malvinas, today we'd be celebrating how we kicked the Brits' asses. So they showed up the next day with the Di Pietro kid safe and sound. And they opened up the trunk. There was that brown *bugre* bitch he was so crazy about. She'd sold him out. 'My gift to you, kid,' Cruz told him. They took her into the back room and put her next to the other guy. Man, did that girl scream. The next day, they went fishing in the Paraná. Let's just say they didn't take any worms with them. I don't know if you kids get it. As part of my payment, Cruz gave me this knife." He hefts it. "That was his way of telling me I was family. Take a good look, kids, because that's who you should look up to. That was Cruz. Not this little shit."

Alina keeps stroking my hand. "I'd like to introduce you to my old man," I'd say if I could find the words. The side door opens, and a black woman comes out looking as Brazilian as anything. Her skin matches the darkness, and she only stands out because of her dress that looks like a set of paint swatches.

"Cruz?" she says. Her accent tells me I was right about where she's from. I nod, and she says in Portuguese, "*O Alvarenga tá aguardando por voce.*"

She turns away and walks over to the bar. She asks the bartender for a whiskey with much ice.

"You're no Cruz," Galarza yells. "Before you go, let's see if you can live up to your last name." With one hand, he lifts up his beergut and shows me the gaucho knife. "I'll be waiting for you."

I open the door, and one last "I'll be waiting for you" disappears behind it when it closes.

# 8.

On the other side is a hallway that's begging for a flash flood of bleach. A construction light shines on a half-open door at the far end. I knock.

"Come on in, *gurí*."

The office looks nothing like the bar or the neighborhood. The grandpa-bathroom-green wallpaper is spotless except for a few humidity bubbles. There's a strong smell of incense trying to cover up all the other odors. An air conditioner purrs. Metal shelves are full of file folders and surrounded by maps and a poster of the Guaraní Antonio Franco soccer lineup from 1981.

"This is an improvement," says Alina.

"I'll be right out," shouts Alvarenga, and I realize that at the other end of the room there are two doors next to each other. The right-hand wall disappears behind a white curtain pocked with cigarrette burns. In the middle of the room is the same desk I remember from Alvarenga's office in Buenos Aires. It looks like a windshield wiper swished across it. One side is covered in odds and ends. The other only has wet newspapers on it.

The door next to the curtain opens and Alvarenga comes out, rolling up the sleeves of a burgundy shirt. The omnipresent cigarrette is camouflaged among the grey hairs above his ear. Two deep wrinkles cut down from his nose toward his mouth like Pancho Villa's moustache. Even the fanny pack looks older. The zippers on the top pocket and his pants are both open. He gives me a bear hug. When he lets go, he sees I'm not alone.

"Well look at you, Tomás. You know how to pick 'em."

"Same to you," she says in a voice with a nervous edge.

Alvarenga laughs. "The Brazilian *garota* used to work in an umbanda temple, but they closed it down and she started turning tricks, so I wanted to help her out. It's tough to lose your faith, even tougher to lose your livelihood." He looks down. "Sorry." He zips up the pocket of the fanny pack. "Excuse me, hon. Alvarenga." He holds out his hand to Alina, who hesitates.

"My hands are dirty."

"I bet they aren't as dirty as mine, sweetie." Alvarenga winks at her.

"Speaking of which," she says. "Is there a bathroom around here where I wouldn't have to kill cockroaches?"

"Use mine." She thinks for a second but ends up going in. "Gorgeous," he says once she closes the bathroom door behind her. "But you should have come alone."

"I'm being followed. A white Isuzu with Paraguay plates."

Alvarenga scratches his cheek, then pulls the cigarette from behind his ear and lights it with his Zippo. He takes a drag. When he pushes aside the curtain, I can see a window that looks out onto a patio. There's a kid sitting in the grass with a Walkman. Another drag. The sound of the toilet flushing in the bathroom. Alina comes out and walks over to us. With his foot, Alvarenga opens a cooler full of ice and booze.

"Grab whatever you want, sweetie. And then would you mind keeping an eye on my grandson for me? His mom's in the hospital taking care of his dad." He looks down and makes it halfway through crossing himself. Alina looks at me, and I nod.

"No problem," she says, grabbing a can of Quilmes. She heads outside and says hi to the kid, who smiles, happy to have someone to play with.

"He's in the hospital because he survived. When I got to the house, he was slapping my daughter around because she hadn't bought beer."

"I didn't know you had kids."

"Six. Not counting you two. Why do you think I've never gotten a new fanny pack?" He leans his ass against the desk and takes a long drag on his cigarette. "When we went to Buenos Aires, I lost contact with everybody. Let's just say I'm not on the best of terms with the mothers. The only one I ever see is this daughter who only wants me to pay the bills when she gets the shit beat out of her by her asshole boyfriend or needs another abortion. The truth is, *gurí*, it's too late for me to be a model father. So the closest thing I can do to the whole dad thing is taking care of her problems."

"When you're not busy fucking a Brazilian chick."

Alvarenga pulls together his fuzzy white eyebrows. He finishes his cigarrette. He turns, finds an ashtray, and stubs it out. He rolls up his sleeves and looks at me.

"If your old man and I believed in God, I'd have been your godfather. Yours and your brother's. And if I wasn't afraid of needles, I'd have tattooed your names on my chest," he says, putting his hand over his heart. "Your old man and me . . . well, the truth is we were more about shooting people than raising kids. But there's one thing we both understand. Enjoying life is an option for most people. If they can't today, then tomorrow. Not us. We're living day to day."

Alina plays with the kid, who lets her listen on one of his headphones.

"The *garota* only works when she's hungry," Alvarenga continues. "So today was my day. Wasn't going to do me any good sitting here and staying *cangú*, crying about your brother. And besides, you know it's good luck to screw a black girl. Now that I think about it, I guess she is still working the faith angle. Hey, don't look at me like that. It's not like I didn't do anything. I got him the best lawyer. He called me today and said the cops are still taking that weed home like doggie bags from a Chinese restaurant. Three to five years, that's it. If he keeps his nose clean, he'll be out in no time."

Alvarenga has gotten back a little of the Misiones accent he'd almost completely lost after years in Buenos Aires. He wanted me to learn what he called *mate*-grower slang so I'd talk like a local. I never picked it up. It was another way of trying not to be anything like my old man.

He puts both his hands on his fanny pack, touching both zippers. Then he leans over, opens a can of Quilmes and passes it over to me, and opens one for himself. He raises the can.

"Cheers, *gurí*."

The beer flows cold down my throat. Alvarenga keeps swallowing until he finishes his, then crushes the can in his hand. The other door opens, and a kid in an Independiente jersey comes in.

"I thought you got lost," Alvarenga says.

"Sorry, boss."

"Any news, Félix?"

"Nope."

"So what do you want?"

"That Brazilian chick was yelling about wanting good whiskey and not that Criadores shit and ended up throwing a glass against the wall. I had to help Parco clean up. That bitch is a handful."

"Wasn't she done making messes after the puddle she left here? It's lucky for me I knew a trick this one's old man taught me." He points at me as he gathers up the newspapers and throws them in the trash. "Since he had these two to take care of, he never took women home. Always in the back seat of the Fairlane. He'd picked up this prissy German girl from the north side of town and when she came, she squirted like crazy. Samuel used to say it was like she had Iguazu Falls between her legs. And the next day, uff. We filled the trunk with catfish, but the smell didn't even come close. So what he did was cover the back seat with a bunch of newspaper. Sometimes you'd see him covered in ink, with the news tattooed on him. Cruz was always front-page shit." He opens the top pocket of the fanny pack. "Except now." He takes out a new cigarette and taps it on the table. Félix looks at him, waiting for the rest of the story. "We grew up together. Like brothers. When he ended up moving to Buenos Aires, I had no choice but to go with him. Now he doesn't want to see me because it'll make him want to go back to the life. He's been offered all kinds of jobs. Even the Di Pietro kid looked him up." He winks at me.

He lifts up a map to show a few pictures of his family. He points out one that was taken almost twenty years ago. Him and my old man, both wearing suits, disposable versions of the two men next to them: the Di Pietros. Senior and Junior.

"Anibal Junior got us into all kinds of shit, man, not a week passed without him making *emboyeré* after *emboyeré*," Alvarenga says. "Two days before this picture was taken, he calls us up screaming. He was balls deep in some bitch coked out of her mind and she passed out. Your old man never told you this story? When we got there, the kid was on the phone making racing bets and the girl was laying there with her nose dripping. We slapped her a couple of times and nothing. Samuel shot her up with some cocktail or other and she woke up. Cruz didn't have an ace up his sleeve, he had a whole goddamn deck. We were about to leave when there's a knock on the door. We get out our pieces, but Anibal says, 'It's cool.' The little bastard had called for another hooker. 'I didn't have a chance to get off with this one,' he says."

"And that guy got elected senator?" says Félix.

"It pays to be born in the right family, kid. Being born into the right family and keeping the right people close. Especially for the shady stuff. He works with Galarza and those boys," he says, nodding toward the bar. "He thought we kept Galarza around because he was tough. Nah. We put up with him because he tells good jokes, but when it comes to work, unless it's just taking somebody out, Galarza doesn't have the brains for it. Anibal Junior wanted to hire us a few different times, but your brother always told him to fuck off. Anyway, why would we, when we were already fine with what we had going on. A little bribe for them and they can be on their way. But nothing big. That's why he called your old man in, *gurí*. He offered him a fortune, a lot of *pirá piré*, but he said no. Those days were over. Said he wanted to get you boys back."

"He never had us, Alvarenga."

"That's not true, *gurí*."

"My brother," I say. "That's why I'm here. What happened? What do I have to do?"

He scratches his neck again. He shoves ice around in the cooler until he finds another beer. Alina's teaching the kid to dance. Alvarenga motions for me to sit and settles himself on the other side of the desk. He touches his fanny pack. He opens the top picket and gives Félix a bag of coke.

"Do an Adidas," he says. Three lines, like the logo. "On the house." He leans back in his recliner and swings it back around to face me. "Your brother . . ." He swivels to one side. Then the other. He sits still. "You probably know your brother and I do import/export of certain products." His eyes move around, showing me different maps on the wall. "Most of these dumb *calandracas* we work with couldn't find blow in Tony Montana's house. And your brother . . . well, he knows it. We brought stuff over in life vests and boat fenders. Kilos and kilos. Until one of those geniuses we worked with drank too much, started acting like a *yurú palangana*, mouthing off. He fucked up a bunch of deals we already had set up. And your brother, instead of stepping back a little, he wanted to work on his own. But he didn't go to the Di Pietros, he got in bed with some other crew. He fucked up. He really fucked up. And now you've got to clean up his mess."

"What do I have to do?"

"A Paraguayan gig."

"What the hell is that?"

Félix lifts up his hand to answer. Alvarenga doesn't even look at him, and says:

"The Centurión crew. You know them?"

"Oh, shit!" says Félix. "Those bastards are tough."

Alvarenga glares at him. Félix looks down at his plate and goes back to scraping out a line.

"Tough is 69-ing with a midget," says Alvarenga. "These guys are something else. I'm telling you this because fear's a good thing, *gurí*. So you'll keep your eyes open. So you won't trust them like your brother did. Cemeteries and prisons are full of people who trusted somebody."

Alvarenga takes a drink of beer. I hear the tap-tap of the razor blade on the plate.

"Are you going to finish your work of art one of these days, Picasso?"

"All set, boss." He comes over with the plate and sets it on the desk. Three lines, all different lengths.

"Go see what's going on."

Alvarenga opens the top pocket of his fanny pack and pulls out a gold straw. He snorts a line. He's going in for the second when the door opens with a bang.

"Ortiz," says Félix. He takes a breath. "Ortiz is slapping around your Brazilian."

They run out. I stand up and try to overhear what's happening. A Paraguayan gig. What the hell does that mean? Out on the patio, the kid's disappeared. Alina's sitting on a wooden table next to a marble one, and there's a well farther back. Remnants of a colonial Jesuit back garden. An oasis. As she comes closer, everything loses its shine and shows its true form. The rusty chairs. The overgrown grass. The well full of mosquito eggs. She's what's different.

Alina leans against the glass and looks at me. The kid appears behind her and stands on his tiptoes to touch her back. He tugs at her hand to show her a puzzle. They turn and walk away. Alvarenga comes back in shaking his right hand and wrapping a towel around his knuckles. In his left hand, he shows me a tooth and puts it in the top pocket of his fanny pack.

"What did you do to Galarza? He says he's going to beat the shit out of you."

"What the fuck is a Paraguayan gig?"

He walks over to the plate and snorts the last line. He squeezes his nose a little. He sniffs. My old man in his room. His runny nose.

"You're going to have to cross over to Paraguay in a boat with some guys who work for the Centurión crew. Everything on the downlow. If the name Cruz comes up at the border, you're going to set off more alarms than a towel-head in the United States. The place is crawling with cops, and Argentine border patrols even worse. When you get there, they're going to give you a job, and you're going to have to do it."

He moves his hand down to the bottom pocket of his fanny pack and takes out a slip of paper. He hands it to me.

"When you're ready, call this number. And *gurí* . . . hurry. That white Isuzu is Centurión's right-hand man. If he's sharking around, it means they're done waiting."

He comes over and puts his left hand on my shoulder as I read the numbers on the paper again and again. The same image almost fifteen years later.

He waves Alina back inside. I rush to put the slip of paper in my pocket.

"How'd you guys do?" Alvarenga asks.

"Your grandson's a real gentleman."

"Just like his grandpa."

"How about you guys?"

"Everything's fine, sweetie." He opens the door next to the bathroom. "Go out this way so you don't run into Galarza. Since I saved her face from getting ruined, my Brazilian lady friend is giving me a second go, and I don't want to pass that up to knock that dumb shit's teeth out."

Alina walks over to the door. My shirt sticks to my back. I can feel the weight of the piece of paper in my pocket like an anchor.

"Tom? Are you okay?" She comes over, takes my hand, and brings me back to the present. "Come on, babe."

My heart's jumping around like a ferret in a bag. Alvarenga zips shut the pocket of his fanny pack. When I walk past him, he whispers:

"Don't worry, *gurí*. You're a Cruz."

**WE GO OUT THROUGH** a metal door next to the bar. We start to cross the road, but halfway across, I let go of Alina's hand.

"Go get in the car. I'll be right there," I say and turn around.

"Tom, where are you going? Stop! Tomás!"

Galarza's still there, behind an army of bottles. It takes him three steps to realize I'm coming for him. He smiles. He's one of those assholes who live for moments like this. Betti pushes her chair away from the table, and her kids stand up. The racket in the bar cuts out like someone pulled the plug. By the time Galarza goes for his gaucho knife, I've already got it in my hand and put it against his throat.

"Stay still, you fuck," I say.

Keeping the knife point against his skin, I turn and get behind his back. We move to face the mirror. His double chin trembles like a toad breathing. I can hear the sound of the fan blades. Then silence. The knife sinks into Galarza's skin. There's a cross carved into the handle. The same one that was on my old man's knives. I push a little. A drop of blood stains the tip of the knife.

"You're lucky I'm a different kind of Cruz."

I take the knife away from his neck and stick it in my belt. Before I shut the door behind me, I look around the bar. If it weren't for the fan blades moving, I'd think I was looking at a picture. Galarza's hands are still in the air.

Alina deflates when she sees me. Her shoulders droop and her eyes close. The paper in my pocket seems lighter. I look to my left and right. The Isuzu's nowhere to be seen. An old man's walking toward me. His head's shaved and he's wearing a green polo shirt and jeans. There are three deep wrinkles cut all the way across his forehead. His huge veins stand out on his arms like snakes. I always thought they had poison running through them instead of blood.

"Wait," he says when he sees me crossing the road. He moves more like a young man than a fifty-year-old. He tries to grab me by the shoulder, but I shake him off. "Tomás. I heard about what happened to Seba."

We look at each other for a few seconds. Two slits that show the brown of his eyes.

"I want to help you," he says. "I want to help you both."

"You already helped us plenty."

"Tomás."

"It's none of your business."

"You're my . . ."

"No," I interrupt him and pull the knife from my belt. He

looks at it. His reflection trembles on the blade. "Of these two things," I say, shaking the blade at him with one hand and hitting my chest with the other, "the only one that's yours is the knife."

I turn it around, leaving the handle toward him, and push it into his stomach. He grabs it, recognizes it.

"Hang on a second, kid. Let me help you."

"If you want to help me . . . Down the road, not across the street," I say, mimicking slitting my wrists.

I turn my back on him and start to walk.

"Tomás. Tomás. Tomás!"

I get in the car and pull away. I don't even look in the mirror. Alina touches my hand on the gear stick.

"Tom," she says, "who was that guy?"

"Someone who used to fuck my mother "

# 9.

My old man never laid a hand on us.

Not even to give us a hug.

The closest he ever came to an affectionate touch was when he fixed up my brother's face after he got beaten up, the summer before my old man was put away.

They told me he'd fallen off his bike. I might have been twelve and looked like an idiot, but I wasn't that stupid. He must have fallen from a bike that was on the fifth floor of a building, I thought. Seba's face was two sizes bigger on account of the bruises. I learned the truth about ten years later when he showed up with his face bleeding again.

This time I had to clean him up. It was when I was still studying medicine and I thought being a doctor was a way of evening things out. Curing injuries to make up for the ones my old man had inflicted.

"What happened to you?" I asked him as I started to clean out his cuts with alcohol.

Seba thought about it, hesitated, and finally started to tell me what had really happened that time he "fell off his bike."

My brother used to play soccer in the lot at the end of a dead-end street. He was usually the youngest one there, and he owned the ball. It wasn't uncommon for him to come home with scrapes and bruises. That afternoon he'd nutmegged the kid who thought he owned the lot: Tonga. He did it once, then a second time. And then a third. Tonga had had enough and punched him. He was five years older and sixty pounds heavier, but Seba didn't back down. He got two punches in before all Tonga's lackeys jumped in and started using him as a ball.

"Samuel got a needle and started to stitch up the cut," Seba said. "While he was stitching me up, I told him what happened and he listened to me. Like he never had before. I swear it didn't even hurt anymore, Tommy. I saw him there, paying attention to me, cleaning me up, and like an idiot I thought I should get beaten up more often so we'd be closer."

Seba never talked about our old man. I didn't even want to think about what he'd done, what had happened to him that was so bad that, instead of telling me about it, he started talking about Samuel. That's what he called him, just Samuel.

"I remember when he was done, he put his hands on my shoulders. That was the closest he ever came to giving me a hug. I even think he was smiling. Then he got all serious and asked where we could find those guys. And then I realized it wasn't a hug at all. He was a trainer massaging his boxer before the fight."

Seba paused and hissed as I pushed the needle into his skin. The cut was deep. It could easily have been a knife cut. An inch lower, and he'd have ended up with an eye patch. I poured on a little more alcohol. The thread went through and was dyed red as the wound oozed. It was the second time I'd sewn someone up. And it was the first time the person was alive. The other time was when they took the med students to cut up dead bodies. A couple of people threw up. Others fainted. I didn't even blink when I had to open them up. Or when I closed them.

I looked at the eyebrow Samuel had stitched up for him. He'd been about as delicate as a butcher. My old man wasn't made to close up wounds in flesh, just to open them. I had to be better, I told myself, and I sewed as carefully as if I were adding the final brushstrokes to a painting. Stitch him up and leave no trace, either of the wound or of my work.

"We went to find Tonga in the bar that was around the corner from the field," Seba went on. "The three of them were there with a few more friends and their girlfriends, leaning on the bar watching a River-Boca game in the summer tournament. We sat down at the other end so we could see them. I was going to ask for a Coke when Samuel stopped me. 'That kind of Coke is for pussies,' he says and orders two beers. We toasted. 'That beer is a fuse, kid. When you finish it, I want you to explode.' He was already on his third when I finished that first bottle. I wasn't afraid. You know, Tommy? With him next to me, I wasn't afraid. He called the manager, said something, and paid him. And then we went to find him. When they saw me they all started laughing. A bartender came over and put down a shot of vodka in front of them.

"'What the hell is this?' says Tonga. 'A gift,' Samuel tells him. 'Look, old man, if you came to make me a peace offering, you should have gotten me a beer. I don't drink this shit.' Samuel laughed in his face. 'That's so they can clean out your cuts and bruises,' he says, pointing at their girl-friends. 'Beat it, old man, we're watching the game.' 'You're watching it because you can't play,' says Samuel. 'With a couple of buddies to back you up, anybody's tough shit. Now we're going to go outside and the two of you are going to fight, one on one. They can't come save your ass.' 'Get out of here or we'll fuck your kid up.' Samuel went over to him and grabbed his shoulder. 'You and him, one on one. Or the three of you against me. And believe me, kid, you wouldn't like that very much.' Tonga smiled and nodded at his six friends to go outside. The girls went, too. Tonga stopped his girl and told her to stay. 'No, babe. You stay here so you won't have nightmares.' 'What do you mean, honey? I love blood.' Samuel stopped her. 'Guainita, it's one thing for you to love seeing blood down there to know you made it one more month without having to go get yourself a garage abor-tion,' he says, looking at her crotch, 'but if you go outside, you're going to end up holding this little prick bleeding like a stuck pig and then you're not going to like it so much.' And I thought, 'I'm fucked.' Because Tonga went red. 'First your kid and then you, motherfucker.' 'To get to me, you've got to beat the kid.' And then he squeezed my shoulders again, and it really was like a bomb. I blew up. There was no way Tonga could get away from me. I ran at him and punched him right in the face. His head bounced off the pavement. I loved that sound. I got distracted, though. Someone kicked me from the side, and I went down. And they kicked me again. Then everybody joined in. I curled up in a ball and tried to kick at them, but I couldn't do a thing. They were kicking me so hard, I didn't even know how many of them there were. I couldn't get my head up. Everything sounded muffled. And then all of a sudden, I could hear again and I understood what they were shouting. 'Stop. Careful. Fuck.' When I opened my eyes, there was only one of them left. He turned and then tripped over me and fell. The sound the back of his head made against the asphalt . . . Crazy. I looked up and saw a hand coming down toward me. It was Da . . . It was Samuel, helping me up."

I had to take a minute because my hand was shaking. The thread trembled between my fingers. My brother looked at me with the eye he could open and then looked down.

"When I stood up, I saw Tonga's girlfriend trying to wake him up," Seba went on. "She was wiping at his face with her hand to get the blood off, and when she wiped her hand on her shirt, she left all five fingers stamped on her white tank top. Another one of the kids who played had his arm hanging off at a weird angle, and the one who'd hit the back of his neck was still out. The other four hesitated, then came at us. The one who came over to me first was a head taller than I was. But I couldn't let him down. I stood my ground and gave him a right hook to the head. When he went down, I smashed his nose, and before I missed all the fun I looked for the other three, but they were already all lying on the ground. Samuel looked at me and smiled. I smiled back, but he got really serious all of a sudden. I got hit in the back. I saw bits of glass flying. I threw my elbow back without thinking about it and connected hard. When I turned around, I saw it was Tonga's girlfriend sitting on the sidewalk, grabbing her broken nose, blood everywhere. The handprint on her tank top disappeared under all that blood, and the stain ended up all the way down between her legs. 'I told you, *guaina*,' said Samuel. 'Tell your man and his friends that if they even think about coming to find us, it's not the hospital we'll send them to next time.' Then he nodded at me and we left. 'You did good, *gurí*,' he said on the walk home."

I put a little more alcohol on his cut and made the last stitch. I tied off the thread and cut it. It was such a perfect suture, it should have been in a museum.

"A few days after that, they called me up for the under-seventeen league. You remember, Tommy, how we started yelling? When I told him, the only thing he said was did I remember to pick up wine. He didn't even look at me. He was watching a race. I told him no, I didn't have time. 'Now what am I going to drink?' he asked. 'Why don't you open one of the bottles from your collection?' I said."

My old man had a nice wine collection in the basement. Mostly presents from his friends in Misiones. Good years. Vega Sicilia '68. Trapiche Malbec '75. Luigi Bosca.

"Only then does he take his eyes off the TV. 'No way. Those are for special occasions. Now go on before Don Blas closes the store.' That was the day I realized he was only interested in problems. Hate was the only thing that we had in common. A shark, Tommy. That's what he is. He's only around when there's blood. And when he finds it, he wants more. And more."

Seba grabbed the mirror and looked at his cut.

"Way better than Samuel," he said. "You're going to be a good doctor."

"What are you going to do, Seba?" I asked him when I saw him heading for the door.

He left without answering.

I stopped studying not long after that. I didn't want to learn any more. I didn't want to end up digging a bullet out of Seba.

My brother was right. As soon as he got out of jail, our old man came to see us. He promised he was going to be straight, that he wanted to be a part of our lives. Seba stood up and told him that if he was part of something, it wasn't our lives, it was our deaths. That if he came back, he was going to show him all the stuff he'd had to learn to settle Samuel's debts.

Samuel could have tried saying he was sorry, but the only thing he said was: "I'm proud of you boys. When you need something, just come find me." And he left. We never saw him again.

That is, until now, when he smells blood and wants more. And I've given him a way to make his wishes come true. I hope he does it.

# 10.

The sounds of the shower stops, and I come back to the present. The TV screen is black. I don't know how long ago the program ended. Alina opens the bathroom door. Her shadow is printed on the wood floor and disappears when she turns the light off. I see her going into the bedroom, wrapped in a towel and combing her hair.

"What's wrong, Tom?"

The drops come together and drip off the end of her hair each time she brings the comb down. Her skin, still wet, shines.

"You can tell me," she insists. "Whatever it is."

I look down. It feels like my tongue is doubling back on itself down my throat. She sits down next to me on the bed. She keeps combing her hair. There's a knot. She keeps at it until she untangles it. We look at each other, and I lean my head against her neck. She puts the comb on top of a box and hugs me. She kisses my forehead. My mouth. My hands move up her legs. Alina pulls her towel off. I go inside her. A shelter of skin. Without Alina, my life would be a religion with no God to worship. I get lost and find myself inside her. And then she lets me go.

The tightness in my chest eases. Our sweat weighs on me like lead. Her head against my shoulder. Her hair falls across her back and half her face. The silence stretches. Not as long as I'd like. Not forever.

"Tell me what's going on, Tom. Or do you think I don't know you're in trouble?"

Her heartbeats start to hammer against my skin stronger and stronger as the silence grows again. The sound of a truck motor. An explosion. I get out of bed. Through the blinds, I can see kids throwing firecrackers. I rub my back against the wall, and chips of paint stick to me.

Alina gets up and sits cross-legged. With two fingers, she puts her hair behind her ears. It falls, covering her nipples, and the ends become shadows on her tummy. The skin becomes white.

"Say something, goddamn it. If I matter to you, open your mouth."

I need you more than ever.

"It's nothing," I say. "My brother screwed up some deals and lost the bar. The guy we went to see is the co-owner, he's trying to see if he can collect some money to open another one."

Sometimes the best thing we can give the people we love

is a lie. She purses her lips. Her reddish hair looks orange. Alina was a woman of iron who went to rust being with me.

"I need . . ." I say.

"What?" She reaches out and strokes my face. "What is it?"

There's only one way to save myself. And I know there's also only one way for her to be safe.

"I need you to leave," I say.

She stops touching me and covers her face with her hands.

"Is that your answer for everything?" I don't say anything. "I can't do anything with that silence of yours, Tom. The rest, whatever it is, you can trust me. But if you don't tell me, I can't help."

"It's fine, Alina. I already told you."

"So why do you want me to leave?"

"I have to go to Paraguay." She squints. "It's the same deal, my brother needs me to take care of a few things while he does some paperwork here."

"Over Christmas?" I nod. "Your brother, your brother. It's always your brother. He moves out here, and you don't even ask me how I feel about it. He gets in trouble, and you don't even think twice about bending over backwards to fix it."

"I don't need this, Alina." My words are lost in the whirlwind of hers.

"When I ask you a question, you can't say or do anything. I came here thinking we could spend the holidays together, but I was wrong again. Where are we going, Tom? Where?"

'Off the rails' would be a good answer. Better and more honest than the silence I give her.

"I'm always the same idiot. I wanted to build something with you. But it's impossible. I'm something you invite into your life after midnight. And I can't keep going like this. You're afraid to let me in. You're a coward."

The "Alina!" I shout is drowned out by the sound of the bathroom door slamming behind her. She's in there for less than a minute before she comes out dressed, pulling down her tank top.

"The last bus to Buenos Aires leaves in half an hour. Hurry up, I don't want to miss it and have to spend Christmas Eve with a bunch of strangers in Gualeguaychú."

"Alina."

"Alina nothing. You asked me to do something and I'm doing it. Now, can you at least do this for me? Or am I asking too much of you?"

I try to hug her, but she pulls away and goes outside. We drive in silence all the way to the bus station. I buy her ticket and look at it. I think about the piece of paper in my pocket. Buy another ticket. Spend the holidays together. Have a family. I walk away from the ticket window. I see her getting a claim ticket for her bag. Alina comes over to me.

"When all this is finished . . ." I say and don't know how to end the sentence.

She doesn't even wait for me to finish. She gives me a kiss on the forehead as if my mouth were another lie. I hand her the ticket. I feel like all that's left of me is my reflection in her green eyes. Her tears start to blur my image. I sink. Her eyes become a stream, they become a river. I'm meat sinking in the Paraná. She leaves. The shore disappears. I'm alone. I sink deeper and deeper. The words I want to say flood my throat, and I drown. With every desperate stroke to keep myself from sinking, my reflection breaks apart, is cut up, goes to pieces. It becomes my brother. I try to kick. I'm nothing. There's no shore. I sink. I drown. The surface moves away. I keep trying to swim. Cutting with my hands. The reflection of my brother comes apart completely. I see what's left. It's not my brother anymore. I'm not me. I'm my old man. I stop struggling. I sink. I drown in the depths of her eyes that disappear behind the curtain, in the depths of those green eyes that can't take another goodbye.

# 11.

Violeta is sitting in the doorway. By her side, her lab Oli starts to wag her tail when she sees me, ruffling my niece's flowered dress.

"Uncle Tommy!" she shouts and gets up. She's so happy running over to me that she pulls Oli along by the leash.

I put down the two bags I'm carrying and bend down to hug her. Her just-washed hair dampens my face, and the apple smell of her shampoo overpowers the smell of the neighbor's fresh-cut grass. Oli pushes her snout into my ribs, demanding a hello. As I pet her, my niece sneaks a peek at the bags until she finds what she's looking for. A red present that says Violeta. She grabs it.

"And just where are you going, young lady?"

"It has my name on it."

"Not yet. Leave that there."

"What is it?" she asks, putting it back in the bag.

"You're going to have to wait till midnight to find out."

She folds her arms. I dig around in one of the bags and give her a Kinder egg that wipes the pout off her face.

"Is Alina going to celebrate with us?" I shake my head. "You're silly, Uncle Tommy. Did you at least get her a present?"

A bus ticket, I think, so the "yes" I tell her is a half-truth. She starts to unwrap the Kinder without letting go of Oli's leash. The dog turns and tangles the leash around Violeta's leg as she tries to bite a piece of the chocolate. It's melting on her fingers. She gives the lab a piece of the wrapper to play with.

"What are you two doing out here?"

Her hair falls across her face, and when she hooks it behind her ear, she smears chocolate across her cheek.

"I wanted to take Oli for a walk, but Mom wouldn't let me. She said she was going to be scared of the firecrackers. But we always walk her and she never gets scared. Not even with the ones that explode a bunch of times."

Two girls go by on bikes, and as they turn into the house on the right, I lose sight of them behind the bushes. My niece finishes the first half of the egg and starts in on the second. Oli checks the silvery wrapper for leftover bits of chocolate. She licks at one. Lelé's hair falls back across her face, and without putting down the egg, she tries to brush it away with the back of her hand. I hook it behind her ear with my finger, and she flashes me a grin with a chocolate mustache. She gives me the orange capsule to open for her.

"I hope it's one of the sharks," she says.

I see some instructions and a couple of loose pieces.

"Oh, it's one of the ones you have to put together." She eats the last piece of chocolate. "Will you put it together for me, Uncle Tommy?"

We sit down on the front step. It's strange that my sister-in-law hasn't come outside yet. I take out the pieces and the instructions.

"A flamingo," she says.

"It's an ostrich."

She shrugs.

"The ones that stick their head in a hole."

"Oh, I know those ones. We saw them on TV the other day. Dad said they hid their heads like that because they were scared."

She sucks the chocolate off one of her fingers. I drop the pieces on the step. The body and the head are blue. The feet and the neck are skintone. There's also a paper tail. I start to put it together. Oli lies down next to me. The neighbor is raking up the grass cuttings and stops to wave to me. It's almost four in the afternoon, but the sky's cloudy and it looks like the sun's about to go down. I can smell the storm in the air.

"Uncle Tommy."

"What, Lelé?"

"Is Daddy okay?"

"Yes, honey. Why?"

"Mom said he was still away. And she started crying. She said it was because she missed him, but she wasn't crying like that. When people cry because they miss somebody, they smile. Mom hasn't laughed in a long time. I showed her some tricks I taught Oli, but she didn't laugh. Look. Come here, Oli. Tell her to sit."

"Okay," I say. "Oli, sit."

The dog obeys and brushes at the grass with her wagging tail.

"Now tell her to shake."

I do, and Oli obeys. My niece looks at me, expecting something. I manage to give her a smile and feel like no matter what it is I have to do, it won't be hard compared to this. I finish putting the ostrich together and hand it to her.

"You're going to have to name it," I tell her.

I bend down and pick up the bags. The front curtain opens. My sister-in-law is looking out. Before I go in, I look at my niece again. She looks like a chocolate clown.

"Come here," I say. "If you get your clothes dirty, your mom's going to be mad at me."

I lick my finger and clean off her face and forehead. I give her a kiss and go inside. Viviana's sitting on the living room couch flipping through a *Gente* magazine with the TV on. I say hi. The smell of cigarettes is overwhelming.

"I brought a few things over in case you need them," I say, holding up the bags. She doesn't answer, so I go into the kitchen and put them on the counter. I put two bottles of

Coke in the fridge along with a Mantecol and some candied peanuts. I take out the cold cuts and white bread. "Do you want a cup of coffee or a sandwich?"

She flips through the channels. *One person injured by a firecracker in Palermo . . . Beat the cream until . . . With two goals by Bruno Marioni . . . In an operation, police arrested . . .* then she changes channels so quickly that I can't even make out the words. I get out a plate and the mayo and make a sandwich for my niece. I cut off the crust and cut the sandwich in half.

"Are you sure you don't want anything?"

"They wouldn't let me see him again," she says. "I went down to the station, and they wouldn't even let me talk to him."

The image on the screen goes still and paints her face white. She's wearing the same clothes she had on yesterday. Her hair looks like an old broom, and the circles under her eyes are dark as bruises. I leave the plate on the counter and go over to her. When I try to put my arms around her, she jumps. She turns off the TV and closes the magazine.

"Did you take care of it yet?"

"I'm working on it."

"What does 'I'm working on it' mean?"

She reaches for the pack of cigarettes. She opens it. It's empty.

"I already went to see Alvarenga."

She looks at me. What I'm saying isn't nearly enough for

her. I grope for something else but can't find any lies she'd believe.

"I have to get in contact with these people."

"So what are you waiting for? The toast at midnight?"

She opens her purse and shuffles through its contents. A bottle of nail polish falls to the floor along with a piece of cardboard holding a row of bobby pins. Her movements are clumsy, and her voice breaks. She must not have slept. She gets up and goes into the bedroom and comes back empty-handed. She goes through the bags I brought with me.

"You didn't stop to think I might need more cigarettes?" She sits back down in front of me and clicks her tongue. "What are you waiting for?" she insists.

Behind her is a shelf with picture frames next to a couple of pencil holders Lelé made in art class. Viviana goes into the kitchen. She opens boxes. The two of them on their honeymoon in Cancún. Seba wrapping my newborn niece in a blanket. The two of us hugging each other as kids. A copy of the original we cut in half when they took my old man away and each of us kept the other, like a holy card. I reach into my pocket. I take out my wallet, a gift from Alina, who was tired of me running around with loose bills in my pockets and constantly losing things. I don't keep money there so much as things I believe in. There are a few pictures of her, a piece of paper with a chocotorta recipe I made the first time she came over. In front of all that, wrinkled and punished by time, the other half of the picture with my brother inside a plastic protector.

"What are you waiting for, Tomás?"

I close my wallet and put it away.

"I wanted to see how you guys were doing."

"They didn't let me see your brother. And I just sit here and stare at that fucking white truck. I had to call the police last night. By the time they got here, it had already left. And do you know what the cop said to me?"

I bite my lips.

"That it wasn't their fault if my husband was in with the wrong people. As soon as they left, the truck came back. So if you want to know how I'm doing . . . I'm scared shitless. So now that you know, why don't you ride off and save the day?"

A car goes by blasting cumbia. She looks around for the ashtray until she finds half a cigarette stubbed out and lights it. She takes a drag. Through the white curtain, the neighbor ties up a bag of grass and leaves it in the garbage bin.

"I know you're not good at talking on the phone," she says and blows smoke in my face. "Do you want me to call and set everything up?" I scratch my neck. She shakes her head. "When the shit hit the fan, your brother didn't think twice about what he had to do, and you . . . you're dicking around. You're an asshole, Tomás."

"Calm down, Vivi."

"You said you were going to take care of it!"

"Stop yelling." I hold up my hands and nod toward the window.

"Coward!" she shouts. I turn toward her. She hits me with both hands on the chest and keeps screaming.

"Calm down," I say again, and I manage to put my arms around her as the anger leaves her and sadness takes over. Her hands encircle my back.

"I can't do this anymore. I can't . . ."

I stroke her hair. She cries. Her face is covered in snot and tears, and I wipe it for her with my shirt.

"It's okay."

Oli starts to bark outside. A dog, I think. I go over to the window but can't see one. Oli barks louder. A car engine starts, and when it roars to life, I recognize it. The white Isuzu. My sister-in-law recognizes it, too. Panic fills her face. I run outside. The truck isn't there. Oli trots over to me alone with her leash hanging from her neck. She looks at me, then turns and barks in the direction the sound of engine drove off. I can't see anything. The bushes block my vision.

"Lelé!"

I run and run and run, but the sidewalk seems not to get any closer, and the row of bushes doesn't end. I dodge Oli. I manage to see the white Isuzu. The red lights come on as it brakes to turn, before disappearing.

Lelé appears next to the bushes, looking at me with fear in her eyes. I let about five pounds of air out of my lungs and feel the blood running through my veins again. Viviana runs past me and hugs her.

"Are you okay, sweetheart?"

Lelé nods.

"A man . . . a man gave me this for Uncle Tommy."

My sister-in-law, without letting Lelé go, looks up at me. I walk over to them. Lelé reaches out her hand and turns it over. Her fingers open like the petals of a flower, leaving behind a crumpled piece of paper. I take it in my fingers and open it.

"What does it say?" Viviana asks. "What does it say?"

Inside, there's a bullet and a note:

*We won't put the next one in her hand.*

# 12.

The day I turned sixteen, a bullet splintered the gate post in the field. The Quilmes cans wobbled, and the birds that were left took flight.

"There's no point," I said, lowering the 9mm, which shook in my hands.

Seba set a bottle on top of the hood of the F100. He straightened his cap and looked at a bus going by on the highway. He took the gun from me and reloaded.

"Aim. Breathe. Shoot," he repeated for the third time, and fired.

The beer can fell on top of a pile. Buried under another pile, sun-bleached, I could see my brother's soccer cleats.

"The problem is that you're looking at the beer cans," Seba said. He fired again. The cans fell one after the other like they were doing the wave. "The key is to think about something you hate and put it there." He handed the gun back to me.

I aimed. My old man "sniffling." I held my breath. My chest wasn't shaking anymore. My old man in jail. I fingered the trigger. My brother's unused cleats. I shot. The can went flying. I turned. A perfect hole in one side and the aluminum torn on the other.

Seba walked over to the truck. He opened the cab and leaned half his body inside. The sun blinded me, and my brother was a dark shape lit from behind. I shaded my eyes with my hands. Seba was bringing over a big box covered in a blanket. He walked over to the gate. Most of his back was drenched in sweat. He set the bottle of Quilmes on the post. Next to it, a bottle of '72 Vega Sicilia. The one my old man kept for a very special occasion. One by one, he set out what was left of Samuel's wine cellar, until the sixteen bottles were lined up on the gate. There were thousands and thousands of pesos sitting there. I only saw targets.

"This one was his favorite," Seba said. He reached into the box again and handed me my old man's Colt 1911. There was a snake etched into the metal, showing its fangs at the mouth of the barrel. The butt was mother-of-pearl with a cross set into it. "Make three wishes. Then blow."

That nothing bad happens to my brother.

A family.

That I never see my old man again.

I aimed at a bottle and pulled the trigger.

———

**A RED MOON SHOWS** through the cables of the bridge that links Posadas to Encarnación. The reflection of its yellowish lights lays bars on the surface of the Paraná.

The last of my old man's boxes were in the garage. That's where he kept the stuff he cared the most about. The Colt chills my hands. I run my fingertip over the scales of the snake that wraps around the barrel like it's trying to squeeze the life out of it. I think about my old man's veins and the gaucho knife I gave him. It was a piece of shit. That's why he gave it to Galarza. But he could still slit his wrists with it. I have his favorite knife tucked into my belt. I shove the Colt into the back of my jeans and cover it with my shirt. I turn over the bullet they gave my niece, then unzip the pocket of my wallet and put it inside, behind the picture of my brother. His face swells, but his eyes are the same, staring at me. Waiting.

*I'm not going to let you down*, I tell him, and try to psyche myself up.

I take out a twenty-five-cent coin. I'm more afraid of that coin than the bullet.

I go into a phone booth.

I dial. I think about what the Paraná must hide. About everything that lives and dies in the water. Someone picks up.

"It's Cruz. Where and when?"


**THE BUS LEAVES ME** on the side of Route 12. Two women get off with me, loaded down with bags that smell like food. A kid takes them and loads them onto the back of a rusty pick-up. The bus disappears around a curve. The mosquitoes start to bite me. I look at the trees in the distance and the darkness beneath them. The women get into the truck and wish me a merry Christmas Eve. I slap a mosquito on my arm. In front of me, a Chevy flashes its lights at me and drives closer.

"Get in," says a kid wearing a Flamengo soccer jersey.

He can barely reach the pedals, and his baby face makes me think he's closer to drinking chocolate milk than beer. There's a machete hanging from his belt. As he drives, he whistles along to a *chamamé*. The gear stick has a Mickey Mouse head. Green splotches cover the windshield as we drive down the dirt road.

"Hang on," he says and jerks the wheel to cut across the grass.

The Chevy jiggles from side to side. We keep going straight until we reach a wall of trees on a rise. I can smell the river when I get out. He nods at me, and I follow him. When we finish climbing the rise, a wooden boat bobbing on the Paraná comes into view. Next to it, a couple of red dots blink on and off. The kid turns on a flashlight and I can see two guys smoking. One's wearing a wifebeater and has a beard that comes down to his stomach. There's a gun tucked into the waist of his shorts. The other one exhales, and the smoke covers his face. I recognize him by his fanny pack. Alvarenga slaps me on the back as I walk by him.

"You took your time, motherfucker," the one with the

beard says, flicking the butt of his cigarette into the river. "Let's go before these goddamn mosquitoes suck me dry."

Flamengo's ready to row. The boat yaws as the one with the beard gets in. I wonder if he's the one from the white Isuzu as I sit down next to Alvarenga.

"Do you know the Pombero? Probably not, because you're a fucking Buenos Aires *porteño*," says the bearded man. "He's the god of the night. Around here, people don't give a fuck about Batman. For them, the real Dark Knight is the Pombero. He's like a Bogeyman, this species of goblin with a huge dick. It's said that if you leave your woman alone, the Pombero shows up, fucks your girl and knocks her up. It's a cheating woman's favorite excuse. Fathers tell their children, 'Behave or the Pombero will come for you.' They tell them that children who misbehave are kidnapped by this creature and then made to disappear in the forest."

"Why are you bringing this up? Are you going to quiz me on local myths?"

"To keep you on track, Little Cruz," he says and shows me a .38. "Mine might not be as pretty as yours, but it's made more people disappear than the Pombero. You get me?"

"Whatever you say, Bogeyman."

"I'm no Bogeyman. You can call me Gamarra."

He sits at the other end of the boat, facing us. Flamengo starts rowing.

"And so you're clear," he says, "people are afraid of the Bogeyman, and the Bogeyman's afraid of Gamarra."

They both smile.

I can make out the other shore, but I feel like it's a lifetime away.

# PART 2
# AFTER
# MIDNIGHT

# 13.

SAMIMBI says the green neon sign that lights up the front of the building and the parked cars. There's a line of people waiting to get in. Parents and kids. Grandmothers and grandkids, lots of grandkids. A red neon sign gives them a second coat of paint: a girl moving up and down a pole in three repeating flashes. That's the prettiest part.

There are bars on every opening, even the tiny windows up near the ceiling. In the parking lot, brand new trucks are parked next to horse-drawn carts. I don't see the Isuzu. A Cimarron in a Santa hat whinnies at us as we walk past it. A couple of the kids in line greet Gamarra like a king. Flamengo says something in Guarani to a girl, and she responds with something else I don't understand, but I'm pretty sure it's not *"Rohayhu."* No one says I love you with a middle finger.

Gamarra waves the bouncer aside, and we go inside.

Near the door is a bar made of a piece of plywood, and a

girl is setting down two plates of pork. The blades of a ceiling fan stripe walls covered in posters of girls in bikinis. Alvarenga walks a few steps behind me. We go down a hallway to a room full of tables with plastic tablecloths. Everyone's guzzling *clericó* and the empty pitchers pile up. A few girls blow kisses to Gamarra. Plates of *sopa paraguaya* and *chipá guazú* are passed from person to person. I don't like anything they're eating. It doesn't remind me of happy times.

We spent the holidays with my old man in Asunción once. We had our midnight toast at eleven because he had to leave early. "Aren't you going to stay and watch the fireworks?" Seba asked. "I've got to set them off," he said and turned on the TV for us. When we got up in the morning, there were a few gifts next to the tree, but they didn't have our names on them. "Which ones are mine?" I asked. "Whichever ones you grab first." Seba left the biggest boxes for me. On one of them I found a tag that said Antonio. "Who's Antonio, Dad?" I said. My old man shrugged and said he was going to sleep. Not to make noise. At the time, I thought the red stain on the tag was wine.

"Let's go, Little Cruz."

The three of them are waiting for me at the back of the bar next to a double door that opens to reveal a livelier environment. Families keep eating as they watch a girl unhook off her bra to the beat of "Rag Doll." I stop short to keep from bumping into a couple of boys who are running to look at a Christmas tree. In the Nativity scene I see the typical

Paraguayan watermelon and coconut flowers. At the table next to it, a father and son share two girls who could easily have been their daughters or sisters, if it weren't for the fact that between them they had about half a pound of clothes, including their little tiaras.

"Around here," says Gamarra, "it's traditional at Christmastime for bosses to give their employees a sweet little bonus."

The doors open again. Two girls come out and give him a hug. On the left is a brunette with a yellow skirt, a blue corset, and a plastic tiara. On the other side is a redhead whose hair looks like it was dyed with crepe paper. She's wearing a bra with two oysters on it that still smell like the sea and green fishnets.

"This is Snow White and the Little Mermaid," he says. The girls give him a kiss on the cheek, and when they're gone Gamarra continues. "A lot of clients and employees came with their families and kids, so we dressed the girls up like Disney princesses. So it's still magical, see?" He holds the door open for us with one hand and sweeps the other through the air to show us the room. "We've got them all. Snow Whites, Cinderellas, Sleeping Beauties. You might even find yourself a Mulan. But if I'm going to be honest with you, they're all Pocahontases here."

On the stage that runs down the middle of the room, a dark-haired Snow White rubs her ass on the pole while Joe Cocker sings "You Can Leave Your Hat On" and she starts to take off her tiara. Disposable princesses here and there. Another Snow White sitting on the lap of a fat man in a Hawaiian shirt, next to a grandmother breaking a *sopa paraguaya* in half and giving it to her granddaughters. The rest of the place isn't much better. Blue lights dye the white walls, and a laser covers them in green spots. The plaster is coming off in chunks like a leper's skin. In some places, the raw brick has been painted. Plastic tables and folding chairs with worn beer logos line both sides of the stage. The place looks like it's full of things they pulled out of the trash. Even the girls. A Mulan and a Little Mermaid smile at us. They've got about ten teeth between them. Mulan tries to grab Alvarenga, but he dodges her.

"Too pale for you?" I say.

"I'm not into Asian chicks."

On this side there aren't nearly as many families, but there are still a few. Lots of men on their own and a father or two showing his son what life has to offer. A brickmaker would take his sons to get mud from the river. A dairy farmer would teach them to milk a cow. These guys bring their sons here.

Gamarra and company go over to one of the circular bars next to the stage. We stay near the pole. The song ends, and the girl picks up guaraníes, reales, and pesos from the floor and tucks them into her thong.

"Where's Centurión?" I ask Gamarra.

He holds up his hands. "Take it easy, Little Cruz. Your brother wasn't the only one who fucked up. Enjoy the show."

He snaps his fingers. "I'd forgotten one. Little Red Riding Whore."

A girl in a red cape and lingerie the same color comes over with a basket in her hands.

"What big teeth you have," she says. "What a long beard you have, and oh," in mock surprise and touching his crotch, she closes with: "what a big cock you have. Are you ready to eat me up, Big Bad Wolf?"

She turns and lifts up her skirt, showing her firm ass. Alvarenga and Flamengo's eyes are about to pop out of their heads.

"Not yet, honey. But we'll take a little bit of this." Gamarra reaches into her basket and pulls out a bag of coke. "Keep on handing it out."

"Are you crazy?" Alvarenga says once Little Red Riding Hood walks away. "Tell me her name, so I can ask Santa for her."

"I wouldn't recommend it. Pretty mouth, but she's a scraper. She'll leave your dick looking like a candy cane."

A guy in a suit and a salmon pink shirt raises his hand at the other end of the room. Gamarra returns the gesture and walks over. He disappears behind a metal door guarded by two men who don't even bother trying to hide the Uzis tucked into their pants.

"Gamarra's a piece of shit," says Alvarenga. "Did you see that girl's ass, *guri*? Not even a touch of cellulitis."

"Alvarenga . . . At that age they don't get cellulitis."

A guy in a Cerro Porteño jersey sits down next to Flamengo. They start to talk in Guarani. They look at us. The kid laughs.

"Do you understand Guarani?" I whisper to Alvarenga.

"Only if it's slow and comes with subtitles."

Cerro Porteño nods at me. "Nice to meet you, *kurepí*," he says.

I don't bother answering. They laugh together. Cerro Porteño slaps Flamengo on the back and leaves. The barmaid gives Alvarenga a whiskey. I order a beer. Flamengo chats with a Little Mermaid who looks like something that really did wash up on the beach. A couple of words and a couple of guaraníes bills later, they walk off hand in hand through a door that leads onto a patio with red fluorescent lights. They should put in a revolving door, I think, seeing the number of people coming in and out. I look back at the metal door. No sign of Gamarra.

"Do you have any idea what we're going to have to do?"

"Does it matter?" Alvarenga says and throws back the whiskey.

I open the can the bartender puts down in front of me and start drinking. *Livin' easy, lovin' free*. A blonde Sleeping Beauty goes over to the rusty pole. After rubbing up on that you'd have to get a tetanus booster. A Little Mermaid collapses on a table. The guy in the suit and pink shirt picks her up by her hair and sends her back to work with a kick in the ass. On the stage, the girl does a couple of clumsy dance moves and ends up grabbing the pole to keep from falling. A Very Sleepy Beauty. They boo her. She looks like she's got a whole pharmacy running through her veins.

"Hey, handsome. What's your name?"

A woman stands by our table, dark hair falling from the tiara like a brushstroke all the way to her waist. A blue dress squeezes her tits and ends high enough to show the tip of a pink thong. She touches the hand I'm holding the beer with.

"What's your name?" she asks again. Judging by her accent, she's from Misiones, not Paraguay.

"Antonio," I say. "You?"

"Don't you recognize me?" she says, and pulls the dress away from her skin, trying to curtsy like a princess. "Cinderella."

She looks at me with her light green eyes. Her makeup is deceiving. She's fourteen, maybe fifteen tops. My chest tightens up like I'm breathing cement.

"It's nice to meet you, Cinderella."

"What would you like me to do for you?" The words sound strange in her mouth, like she's lip-syncing.

"How old are you?"

Now it's her turn to hesitate. Alvarenga whispers in my ear: "Go for it, idiot."

"For the right price, I can be any age you want."

I shake my head. Her hands double down and move toward me again. They're shaking. She tries to lift up my shirt, and she jumps when she feels the Colt sticking out of my waistband.

"And what are you going to turn into after midnight?" Alvarenga asks, craning his head over my shoulder. I slap him away. She looks up.

"It's always after midnight here," she says.

I think about Alina. Someone you invite over after midnight.

The girl looks at the floor and wiggles her feet from side to side. No glass slippers. This is a Cinderella in white sneakers stained with red dust.

"Get back to work," says Gamarra, handing her to a kid who's licking his lips. The kid leads her to the doors at the back. "We'll have her ass looking like a pumpkin after midnight."

"Where's Centurión?" I say, but Gamarra walks away again into the crowd, which parts for him.

A drunk guy passes out on the bar. Alvarenga reaches over and steals his pitcher of *clericó*. He pours himself a cup and holds the pitcher out to me. I shake my head. The Very Sleepy Beauty takes off her bra to show a nice pair of tits. She rubs them against the pole and a few more flakes of rust fall off. When she turns, she gets her leg tangled with the pole and falls to the floor. One of the guys in suits carries her away. Alvarenga slaps me on the back and signals that he's going to the bathroom.

Gamarra passes near me and I grab his arm.

"Listen to me. What the fuck are you doing?"

He shakes me off. He looks around and then sits down on the stool where Alvarenga was.

"Let's see if we understand each other, Little Cruz. We had to wait two days for you. Now it's your turn to wait." He puts his hands on my upper arms and whispers in my ear. "You got the good end of the deal because right now you've got something nicer to look at than a fucking glove box. Although your sister-in-law's pretty easy on the eyes." I feel the muzzle of his gun against my stomach and stand up straighter. "Your niece, too. How old is she? Ten, eleven? Another year or so and she could start working for us."

"You son of a bitch."

"And proud of it. So if you don't want your niece to become a pretty little princess, shut the fuck up and wait."

He winks at me and disappears. It takes me a minute to start breathing again, and when I let the air out, my chest falls to my knees. My hands shake, and I put them on the Colt and the knife. A sudden calm is injected into my bloodstream.

"That one was your old man's favorite," Alvarenga says. "He really took care of it. Before he used it, he'd always take it apart and oil it up."

"If he'd done half as good a job taking care of us . . . we wouldn't be here."

I cover up the Colt with my shirt and ask the barmaid for another beer.

"Why the hell are you here?" I say.

Alvarenga lets out a long breath. He spins around the damp glass.

"Well?"

"Your old man sent me to protect you."

"He thought of that too late."

"Don't say that. It was your brother who fucked everything up, not sure if you caught that part. And if your old man wants . . ."

"I don't give a shit what he wants. Why don't you go fuck some girl and leave me alone? They must have a Brazilian around somewhere."

"Fuck you, *guri*," he says, getting up.

"Fuck you too."

The first chords of "Crazy" come over the speakers. Very Sleepy Beauty comes back out and does a few moves with Mulan.

"I thought Asian girls were skinny. Look at that tub of shit!" someone shouts.

The girl doesn't say anything. She probably can't understand him. When she comes closer, I can see that Very Sleepy Beauty has two pieces of bloody cotton balls in her nostrils that match the maxipad sticking out of Mulan's thong. I want to throw up. I swallow the bile. I hang my head. I retch. I breathe in, then out. It passes. Just barely. I squeeze the empty beer can. The aluminum cuts my skin and I see blood.

"Careful, all our first aid kit has is morning-after pills."

Cinderella has replaced Alvarenga next to me. She straightens her dress, and instead of facing me, she points her knees toward the bar so her thong won't show below the hem of her skirt.

"Since you're a gentleman," she says, "would you buy me a drink?"

"Sitting around wasting time again?" The guy in the salmon pink shirt grabs her by the arm. "Get in back, there are people waiting."

She gives me a look.

"She's with me," I tell him and signal the barmaid to get her a drink.

The guy looks at me, then her, then lets go of her arm.

"Thanks," she says and sips the orange juice the barmaid gives her. "You pay for a screwdriver and they give you watered-down Tang," Alvarenga had told me. Her tiara is crooked. I straighten it for her. She looks down at her feet.

"There weren't any shoes my size," she says.

"Blue looks nice on you. It matches your eyes."

"They're the only nice thing Marina gave me." She takes another drink. She touches my face, and her hands are cold. "*Nde resa porã.*" I frown. She throws back the rest of the juice. "I said you have pretty eyes, too. Pretty, but sad. Do you want me to make you happy?"

I sigh.

"What's wrong? Do you like Snow Whites better?"

"Princesses aren't my type."

"That's good, because I'm a queen." She looks around her. The guy who was asleep on the bar has thrown up, and there's a puddle around his face. "And it looks like you're the only Prince Charming in here."

"I'm no Prince Charming."

She puts her untied sneaker on the stool between my legs. The laces are frayed. I tie a bow and tighten it.

"In the story, everybody wanted to be Cinderella," she says. "When the prince went to find the fairy godmother, the stepsisters cut off their toes and heels so the shoe would fit."

"That's not what happens in the movie."

"That's in the original version."

"I don't know it."

The barmaid takes Cinderella's empty glass and looks at me. I nod, and she serves her another.

"When I was little, Marina never read us stories," she says. "She never did anything, really. Just abandoned us. When she left, my sister read me the original versions. So I'd understand, so neither of us were stupid enough to believe in fairy tales. You know?"

My throat's dry, and I want to order another beer, but the barmaid is busy.

"And in the end, I turned out to be a princess."

She looks at the floor again. Her face disappears behind the curtain of her hair. She rubs her eyes. Someone grabs my shoulders from behind.

"You got your wish, Little Cruz," says Gamarra. "Centurión's waiting for you. Let's go. And you get in the back, girl."

Cinderella and I look at each other for a moment. Then we look down and each let ourselves be dragged off.

# 14.

Gamarra shoves me into a warehouse. It's full of tables with chairs turned upside down on top of them and beer crates piled in a corner. Vines of wiring climb the rusty beams that hold up the sheet metal roof. The seams between rotten sheets of wallpaper trace black lines down the walls, and the metal of the upturned chair legs fills the space with bars. It's like they're putting me in prison.

A fluorescent bulb flickers above a table covered in a forest of beer bottles. Flies buzz over bits of food. There's a guy in a Chicago Bulls number 13 jersey sitting in a chair stamped with a Polar logo, picking dirt from under his fingernails with a pocket knife. In the back are two other men staring at the floor. The taller of the two can't be more than five foot seven. He's wearing a sun-faded brown cap and a polo shirt full of holes that hasn't been white in years. Either he's got a serious case of pinkeye or just smoked a pound of weed. The other one's shirtless. His long black hair flutters when a fan that looks like the propeller of a dive bomber hits him from the right. His tanned skin is covered in tattoos. There's a Gauchito Gil on one pec and Olympic rings on the other. None of the three guys look at me. None of them looks like Centurión. They only move their heads when a scream comes from the far side of the warehouse, and all of them look at a painted metal door.

"Your piece," says Gamarra.

I move my hand to my waist. I take out the clip and put it on the table.

"What about the one in the chamber?"

Flies crawl over a pork bone. Chicago Bulls pushes back the cuticle on his index finger with the handle of his knife. The one in the cap rubs his elbow, and his buddy shakes his left leg like someone's electrocuting him. A door slams. Footsteps come closer.

"So, Little Cruz?"

The metal door opens.

"He's not going to do anything with one bullet, Gamarra," says the guy who appears. "If it was his old man, we'd have to pull out his teeth to say he was unarmed."

Where his head isn't bald, patches of grey hair stick out like tufts of grass covered in snow. There's still some black left in his goatee. Shorts and flip-flops. His sand-colored shirt is unbuttoned, showing a scar across his chest. Judging by his arms, he must have been a boxer. Judging by his crooked nose, he's been in a few fights. And judging by his bloody hands, he just came from one. Centurión wipes his face with a rag and throws it on the table, sending up a cloud of flies.

"Silent Night's just a song today. It took some doing, but the motherfucker talked," he says, passing Gamarra a fold of paper. "Off you go."

"What about this guy?"

"We're not going to have any trouble with this Cruz."

Gamarra goes out the way we came in. The other three act like nothing happened. Centurión motions for me to sit down.

"I always wanted to work with your old man," he says. "I invested the first money I earned in a couple of *mate* fields I managed from Buenos Aires. I never really knew shit about harvesting, but around the mid-80s I realized the real money wasn't in *mate*, it was in weed. And to switch over to that business I needed people from around here who already knew it. People like Samuel Cruz. When he moved to Buenos Aires, I said, 'This is my chance,' and I started to track him down. Tough guy to find, your old man. I was about ready to throw in the towel when I found out your old man was going to play for the U-17 team in the game against Colombia. No way he was going to miss that. I was pretty pissed when I didn't see him there. I'd even say I'd spent a ton of money for nothing, except it was a great game. Your brother kicked ass. Two goals. Little bastard was a powerhouse. And on top of talent, he had a good head. On the field, and off." He checks a bottle of beer. La Diosa says the label. He jiggles another. And another. All empty. "In the end I couldn't work with your old man, but I worked with a Cruz. And we did pretty damn well. But as talented as he was, your brother always had a problem. He kept getting caught offsides. On the field, and off."

He continues checking the bottles in the middle of the table. He kicks the guy in the Bulls jersey.

"Finish your fucking manicure and get me something to drink."

The kid puts away his knife, and as he walks over to a freezer, I see that on his back, above the number 13, it says Longley. The clip from the Colt shines on top of the table. With his right hand, Centurión opens his shirt and shows me a chrome Smith & Wesson. Chicago Bulls comes back with a bottle of beer. There's something stuck to the glass, and only when Centurión picks it off do I realize it's a piece of bloody flesh.

"Don't worry about sticking this last one in there. That asshole's going right in the river," he says, tossing his head in the direction of the metal door. Then, looking at me, he says, "That's my boy, Sherman. The biggest one. And the deafest. I told him to use a knife to take a guy out, and what does this one do? He goes and blows him to bits with a shotgun. Can you believe that? Three hundred pounds of ground beef making a mess on the floor. I almost got a fucking hernia shoveling it into the freezer, and now all my beer bottles come with surprises."

He scratches another piece off the bottle.

"Next time the knife. You got that, kid?"

Sherman smiles, and his father pours himself some beer and offers me the bottle. I raise my hand to turn him down. I wonder how Seba ended up working with these people.

"It sucks what happened to your brother," says Centurión. "But don't feel bad, it happens to the best of us." He points at the two guys at the back of the warehouse. The one with the tattoos starts to move both his legs. The one in the cap keeps scratching his elbow. If he keeps up like that, we'll be able to see his bone in a couple of minutes. "The Jap and Mateo Docabo. Cousins. Both won gold medals in rowing in the Panamerican Games in '95. They're talented bastards, too. Give them a boat and they'll row it across the ocean and back like it's nothing."

The taller of the two pulls his cap down to his ears. The other one puts is hand over the Gauchito Gil tattoo as if he were singing the national anthem.

"But there's no money in rowing in this country. There's money for you if you're a junkie, or if you pop out kid after kid like taking a shit, but if you've got talent and could really go far, you can't get a fucking cent. So the Docabo boys know how to row and need a future. Need it bad. The Jap," he says, pointing to the one in the cap, "smokes so much he's making weed an endangered species. He also likes his blow. One time he was hurting for cash and he sold the gold medal, ounce by ounce. I hated to see so much talent go to waste. So

I gave them a job they can be good at. You should see those boys row. It's art. Charlton Heston in *Ben Hur* looks like a worm compared to these two. Until one day Soto calls me and says, 'Look, Centurión, the shipment's short.'"

"We . . . we got jumped," the one in the cap mutters.

Centurión raises his hands in a shrug. "And what about the two times before that?" The guys don't answer. "My buddy in there told me everything about this trip," he says, pointing toward the door. "I'll deal with them later. Right now I'm talking to you two."

Mateo is scratching at the Gauchito Gil on his chest. Now his cousin has stopped itching himself and starts to shake his legs, like they've switched roles. Centurión finishes off the beer and grimaces. He motions to Sherman, who gets up and goes over to the freezer. Gamarra comes back in the door we first came through.

"All set, boss," he says and sits down next to me.

He takes the little paper still covered in coke from his pocket and rubs it across his teeth like dental floss. Sherman drags over a table with wheels. On top of it, a sheet covers something square. Centurión stands up and pulls it off. Underneath is a scale with two trays. The lower one has few weights on it. Next to the scale there are bullets and bills.

"Two ounces for the whole job," says Centurión. "Soto told me they only took half, so . . ." He takes off two weights. "One ounce of cash."

He starts to put bills on the other tray. Pesos pile on top

of each other. The Jap sniffs, and his chest shrinks to half its size when he lets the air out. Centurión adds a few more, and the trays come even. He takes the bills off and puts them down to one side.

"The other ounce has to be in lead," he says, and puts three bullets on the tray.

A stain darkens the Jap's pant leg, and as it grows, it becomes a river.

"No, boss," says Mateo. "We won't let you down again."

Gamarra pats me on the back.

"Don't do it, boss," Mateo insists. "We're going do you right. Please. I'm begging you. I've got a family. I've got daughters."

"A deal's a deal," says Centurión. "Time for the lead medal." And he shoots the Jap.

The shot in his chest stamps him against the back wall. The second one to his head sprays his brains across it. He starts to fall to the side, and as he slides down, his blown-out skull and back paint two lines. The smoking Smith & Wesson points toward Mateo, who's crouching with his head hidden behind his arms. By the time the Jap hits the floor, two rainbows of blood are painted across the wallpaper.

Centurión moves the barrel closer to Mateo's head.

"Look at me, you pussy," he says.

The puddle of the Jap's piss mingles with his blood.

"I told you to look at me. I like it better that way. Now get up."

His legs tremble. He looks to one side to keep from seeing his cousin.

"You've got two daughters and I've got one bullet. What do you say we trade?" Centurión lowers his gun. "I saw your girls a while ago. They're pretty. Good thing they took after their mom instead of you. How old's the older one? Seventeen?"

Mateo can't stop shaking. It's hard to say whether the movement of his head was a nod.

"And the other one? Fifteen?"

"Th . . . thirteen."

"Young . . . but not too young. Let's do this, Docabo." Centurión moves closer to Mateo and puts a hand on his shoulder. "I don't know what it is, the Christmas fucking spirit, but I'm feeling generous. I'm going to make you an offer you can refuse, but I wouldn't recommend it. If you want me to hang onto this bullet, you aren't going to have arms anymore, just oars. And you're going to pick one of your little girls to work for me until she swallows a whole Paraná River of cum."

A piece of brain falls off the wall and lands on top of its former owner. Mateo shakes his head, and drops of sweat fly off in all directions.

"It's hard for a father to choose his favorite kid, but it's also hard to run a business when your employees are a bunch of fuck-ups. You can see I'm a fair guy," he says, jerking his thumb at the scale. "It's a simple equation. Two Docabos are going to work for me. Gamarra's going to walk you to your table, and you're going to give him whichever of the two you choose. If you say no, he'll plug you right there and they'll both end up working for me. Make it a Christmas present and save one of them."

Mateo bites his lips. Gamarra grabs him by the back of the neck and herds him out, just like he herded me in here. A couple of tears fall to Mateo's chest, and it looks like Gauchito Gil is crying. Centurión puts the Smith & Wesson back in his belt. He walks over to the freezer and opens it.

"Not a single fucking Quilmes," he says, shaking a bottle of La Diosa at me. "This shit tastes like piss. I think Paraguayans don't have a sense of taste, Cruz. They got rid of it to keep from going extinct. Have you seen Paraguayan women? Horrible. Docabo's daughters are cows in Argentina, but here they're fucking supermodels." He comes back to the table with a beer in his hand. He takes a drink from the bottle and grunts to get it down. "I hope that dumb shit chooses the thirteen-year-old."

Sherman stretches and looks at the Jap. Half his face is submerged in blood.

"Good thing you told me to use a knife," Sherman says.

"You have to honor deals, kid. If I promised lead, it's lead. That goes for you, too, Cruz."

He sits down. The flies leave the bone behind and head over to visit Docabo.

"What do I have to do, Centurión?"

The father and son exchange a look.

"Well, who knew, he speaks."

"I don't know how long your brother's going to be out of play," Centurión says, "but you've got to fill in for him this game." He takes another drink of beer. "You used to be able to trust people. When they made a promise, they kept it. Now with all this bullshit going on in the country, it's tough to find men of their word like me. And those lying sacks of shit are fucking it up for the rest of us. That asshole we've got for a president came out and said whoever made a deposit in dollars would get dollars back, and then everything went to hell.

"Up until a few months ago we were working with some powerful people—suits, cops. You gave them a few pesos and nobody saw anything. On you go, nothing to see here. They had their own side gigs. But the problem is these guys heard the president and said, 'We want to keep earning dollars.' And they didn't really want to take no for an answer. They started to bust my balls, attack my shipments or come and cut down my fields, or shoot them up. The border patrol never used to show up anywhere, and now they've got so many goddamn boats on the river this place is starting to look like Venice.

"The guy I was chatting with when you came in, other than spilling about a half gallon of blood, told me where these guys have their camp. We're going to show them the Centurión crew doesn't work in pesos or dollars. We work in blood. And it's time to collect. That's your job, Cruz." He pours me some beer. "Cheers."

We toast with plastic cups. I don't know if the beer is terrible or good. I drink. It's an hour and a half till Christmas.

I wonder who the hell I'll be after midnight.

Centurión gives me back my clip. I grab it, but he doesn't let it go.

"Don't let me down, Cruz. Don't be like your brother. Be like your old man."

I yank at the clip until he lets go. I've barely finished putting it back into my Colt when the door swings wide open. Gamarra pushes in two girls by the back of the neck. The taller one is blonde. The younger one has two dark braids that fall to either side of her face. Along with tears, the girls' dresses are spattered with blood.

"Docabo couldn't pick," he says.

Centurión rubs his hands together.

"Initiative," he says. "I like that."

"What costume should I give them?" Sherman asks.

"Turn them around."

His son spins them around and lifts up their dresses to show his father their asses. The brunette's wearing a black thong. The blonde's wearing a red one.

"With those apple cheeks, give the younger one the Snow White outfit. And give the other one whatever we've got lying around. She won't have it on long, anyway. Are you guys ready?" he asks Gamarra.

"All set."

"Go on, Cruz. I hope your brother's shoes aren't too big

for you to fill. Because if they are, other people in your family are going to have to try them on. Either the girls here, or that pretty little thing from Buenos Aires."

I grit my teeth and taste blood in my mouth. Gamarra looks at his elbow, notices he's got some Mateo on him, and wipes it off on the older girl's dress.

Sick fucks.

"Wait, kid," Centurión says to his son. "Leave me the little one as a Christmas present. Although I don't think I can wait til midnight to open her up."

"Come on," says Gamarra.

We go out into the hallway. The doors close, the crying and screaming on one side, the music and Disney princesses on the other.

Gamarra stops, turns to face me, and grabs me by the shoulders. "Little Cruz," he says. "Next time I ask you for something, you give it to me. Whether it's a beer or the bullet in the chamber. You give it to me. Don't tell me no."

"You know what, Gamarra? You won't want me to give it to you."

"Why?"

"Because I won't be putting it in your hand."

"Hey, champ, don't steal my line"

He looks at the barrel of the Colt and smiles.

"Now we're starting to understand each other. You're turning out to be a real tiger's son."

"A tiger's brother," I say, and we start walking.

# 15.

The white Isuzu bounces as we move through the hills. In the back, Alvarenga and I hang on to the side to keep from falling out. Nearer to the cab, Gamarra scratches his knee with the barrel of his Beretta. Next to him is a guy named Tagui. He has a goatee, a striped polo shirt, and a double-barrell shotgun that looks like a lighter in his hands. He takes a snort and passes the packet of coke to Gamarra. Alvarenga finishes his cigarette and throws the butt away. Ahead of us, the light of the cab is all we can see. Flamengo drives, singing a *chamamé*. Cerro Porteño joins in for the chorus. A few fireworks cross the silvery clouds ahead of midnight.

The road snakes and disappears. Beyond a field fenced in by trees, the forest becomes a jungle. The weeds are higher than the hood of the truck. Broken branches and leaves get caught on the cab. The dust sticks to my sweaty hands, and I wipe them on my jeans again. The tail lights paint the weeds red behind us. The Isuzu is like an animal leaving a trail of blood behind it.

Gamarra bangs his hand on the roof of the cab, and Flamengo brakes. Without the buzz of the engine, it seems like someone's turned up the volume on the animal noises. Clouds of mosquitoes attack us in spite of the gallons of repellent we've put on. Something breaks from the underbrush and runs off.

"Go have a look around, Tagui," says Gamarra. While Tagui walks up to the top of the hill, the rest of us pile out.

Gamarra leans against the door and finishes off the coke. Flamengo starts talking in Guarani with Cerro Porteño. A gust of wind cools the sweat on my back. Tagui disappears into the trees. The leaves rustle and look like a million butterflies moving their wings.

"Like it or not, I made a promise to your old man," Alvarenga says, cocking his gun.

Gamarra, his legs crossed in front of the bug-filled grill of the Isuzu, looks at me.

"We'll see if you're as tough out here," he says. "Hate to see you pussy out."

I spit on the ground and take the Colt out of my waistband. Flamengo sticks two fingers under Cerro Porteño's nose, and he throws his head back.

"Damn," he says. "That Little Mermaid spent too long underwater. You fucked up there, *caputi*. You should have gone with the Cinderella who was talking to that *kurepí*."

He points at me, then closes his eyes and bites his lip. "That *yiyi* has such a tight little *cashi* you've got to shove to get it in." Flamengo and Gamarra snort. "Why isn't this *quirapai* laughing?"

I picture Alina dressed up as Sleeping Beauty and Violeta as Tinker Bell. I want to spit again, but my mouth's too dry.

"He's scared," says Gamarra.

Tagui waves to us from the trees.

"Let's go," says Gamarra, and we start walking.

The Paraguayans go first. Alvarenga and I are in the middle, and Gamarra brings up the rear. I try to keep up with him. My fingers slip on the metal scales engraved in the Colt. I take it in my left hand and wipe my right on my pants. The ground is a wet cushion of plants. Shards of moonlight cut out pieces of us in the darkness. The 9mm tuck into Cerro Porteño's waistband. The back of Alvarenga's neck, the cigarette behind his ear. The Colt, shining white like it's made of bone. Leaning against the last tree trunk, Tagui's shadow. He puts out his arm and points at the camp on the slope.

All around it are hundreds of marijuana plants a yard high. In the middle, the grass disappears and gives way to dirt, and there's a cabin painted blue. The light coming out of the windows prints yellow squares on the ground. To the right is a tunnel with a tarp roof. Where it's been pulled back, upturned U's of wood show through like the ribs of an enormous skeleton. Inside are burlap sacks. Farther back is an extended-cab Chevy truck and another smaller tunnel. At the end, two shacks with sugarcane walls. Then the jungle swallows everything up again.

"No one fires until I give the order. Got it?" says Gamarra. He nods and we start down.

We leave the weeds behind and walk into the marijuana plants. Cerro Porteño cuts off some buds and puts them in his pocket. The dust has settled on me like a second skin. My fingers start to cramp up from squeezing the Colt so tight. Gamarra raises his hand, and we stop. I breathe through my mouth.

"Easy," Alvarenga whispers to me.

We're in front of the tunnel. I can hear voices speaking in Guarani from inside. From the wooden braces where there's no awning, marijuana plants hang upside-down like animals bleeding out. The front door opens. A guy with no shirt on. Shorts and flip-flops, a gun sticking out of his waistband. He shouts in our direction. I can't understand what he says. He goes into the tunnel, and we lose sight of him behind the tarp. Somone from inside answers him. Gamarra taps his ear and looks at Flamengo, who shakes his head.

"They are just talking shit," he says.

Gamarra and Tagui signal each other with their hands. The guy comes back out and stands next to the dry plants. He lights a cigarette. Flamengo raises his piece, and Gamarra pushes his hand down. "Calm the fuck down," he says in such a low voice that I read his lips more than hear him. My chest closes up like I'm breathing in smoke. The guy takes a drag and looks up at the sky. A noise comes from inside the cabin. He takes a final drag and throws away the cigarette.

There's an explosion, then another a second later. The first, a firework, lights up the hills farther back. The second is Flamengo's gun. The shot hits the guy in the chest, and he falls backwards.

"Goddamn it," says Gamarra and starts to run for the tunnel. "God fucking damn it."

The guy tries to get up until another shot explodes his head. I can hear shouts in Guarani. Alvarenga grabs my shirt and signals to me that we should head around back. Tagui sprays the tarp with buckshot. A couple of support beams come loose, and the roof falls. The silhouettes of three men appear like ghosts made of garbage bags. They try to raise their arms, but the tarp weighs them down. A shot takes one of them out. A shotgun round drops another.

"Let's go, *gurí*," shouts Alvarenga.

We head for the two shacks at the back. The first tunnel disappears behind the smaller one. Gamarra and the Paraguayans reach the door of the cabin. Tagui fires the shotgun. Splinters and screams.

Flashes light up the inside of the cabin, and the light printed on the grass goes whiter. Broken glass. More flashes. The smoke from the gunpowder makes my nose itch. Through the back window, a set of Christmas lights splash the ground with pulsing blue and red. A doorway appears in the darkness, and when the lights go out, it disappears. We reach one of the shacks. Between us, one of the cane walls splinters, and then the smoke comes out. The blue and red pulsing illuminates the doorway and the guy shooting at us. More splintering. Alvarenga shoves me.

"Get back, get back," he shouts, returning fire.

We hide behind the other shack. I crane my neck. The Paraguayan's shots move away toward the plants on the other side.

"Shoot, *gurí*. Cork him." Alvarenga says and starts running after him, still firing.

I pull the trigger without aiming. The shots continue from inside and outside the house. The air's filled with dust and gunsmoke. The blue and red pulse again. A shotgun fires. The windowpane shatters and bits of a person fly out and land in the dirt. On the pieces of glass left in the window-frame, the pieces of flesh and blood slide and fall on the sill, piling up like horse shit.

Alvarenga disappears into the marijuana plants, and the explosions from his gun move off down the slope. I inch forward along the wall of the shack toward the house. I want to listen, but the sound of my breathing drowns out all the other noises. I hold my breath. Voices. Close. Very close. My lungs beg for air. I give it to them. The noise of guns. I hold my breath again. Yes. It's voices. Someone opens the door of the first shack with the muzzle of a gun. He comes running out. I pull the trigger. The cane door explodes. He turns and takes a shot at me one-handed. His arm is thrown back by the kick. He loses his balance. The shot hits him in the chest and turns him around. He falls face first on the ground. His revolver skitters away and I lose sight of it in the dark. The guy rolls over. The blue and red pulse broadens his shadow, and his skin goes purple. His stomach is covered with dirt. He tries to stop the blood flowing from his chest. He says something in Guarani I can't understand.

"Shut up, asshole. Shut up and don't move," I say.

He keeps repeating the same words.

"Shut the fuck up." I take a step forward. The sweat's pouring down my face.

"*Taita!*"

The shout comes from the shack. The person running out is also shirtless. I raise my gun. He turns his head. It's a kid. My finger shakes on the trigger. The Christmas lights go out. Darkness. He has something in his hand.

"Don't move!" I say and keep my gun trained on him. More shouting in Guarani. "Nobody fucking move! Stay right where you are, kid."

The blue and red pulsing comes back. His mouth is twisted. His eyes and skin shine. In his right hand is a machete bigger than he is. He comes at me. A rosary bounces against his chest as he runs.

"Stay the fuck where you are!"

He lifts the machete. I close my eyes. The lights blink back on and shine on him like the lights on a cop car. That kid is me the night they took my old man away. My eyes burn. My nose burns. Everything burns. I aim. I shoot. I miss the first time. And the second time. The third shot hits him. It takes off two of his fingers. The kid falls backwards, and the machete flies forward, landing at my feet. Next to him on the ground are two worms made of meat: his thumb and another finger. With his good hand, he grabs at his glove of blood.

"*Taita*," he keeps shouting, crying.

The guy who must be his grandfather shouts back in Guarani, his voice high through his tears. His arms are flung wide, and he's looking at the sky. Alvarenga comes back from the hill with one gun in his hand and another tucked into his pants. He doesn't even bother to look at the two Paraguayans. He puts a hand on my shoulder, and I jump as if he'd startled me.

"Take it easy," he says. "Take it easy. And you too, you little shit. Don't move," he says and coldcocks the kid.

A scream comes from the other side of the house. Gamarra leans out, recognizes us, and starts to come over. A shard of glass falls from the windowframe at the back. Inside, I can see two legs in a pool of blood and a broken high heel. Flamengo and Cerro drag Tagui with them. They lean him against the side of one of the shacks. His chest is a mess. He coughs.

"Can we do anything for him?" Gamarra asks Alvarenga.

"Make it quicker."

Gamarra walks over, looks at Tagui, and in a single movement takes out his Beretta and puts two bullets in his head, which spins to the side and spits two ropes of red on the moss-green wood.

Cerro Porteño bends down and puts one of the marijuana flowers he stole on Tagui's chest. He bites his knuckles and closes his eyes. The silence is ruptured by the shouts of the Paraguayan I shot, who's writhing around like a worm. Gamarra looks at me. He grabs Tagui's shotgun and turns toward them. The kids starts to back away like a crab, trying to escape. He hides behind his hands. The grandfather shouts. He tries to get up. He's pale and weak. Gamarra stands in front of the kid. The buckshot tears through the boy's fingers and face. The father curls into a ball. He lies face-down, and his crying is smothered by the ground. Gamarra rests the barrel against the back of his head. He pulls the trigger. His head comes apart like he swallowed a grenade.

"That's how you do it, you little fuck," he says. His beard is covered in blood and bits of flesh. "Get the weed and load it up."

I get lost staring at the hole in the father's head.

When I regain something like consciousness, I'm putting down a bag full of bricks of marijuana in the back of the Isuzu. I step over a body and grab another full sack. Alvarenga comes over and shakes down one of the dead men. He looks around and then gives me a handful of bills.

"Let's grab what we can." I stuff them quickly into my pocket and stare at the dead man. "We couldn't leave any of them alive."

"What?"

"Look." He touches a brick of marijuana with his foot, showing me the horse logo on it. "This is Di Pietro's. If someone got word to him, what we did to these guys would be a blowjob from an angel compared to what they'd do to us. A real genius, your brother."

He leans over and throws a sack over his shoulder. We get into the truck. Along with the weed, there are a few Christmas presents in the back. One of the tags says Felipe. Another's for Mercedes. I wonder who took care of the kids. Alvarenga takes the cigarette from behind his ear and lights it. The Isuzu starts up, followed by the Chevy. Fireworks continue to light up the night.

# 16.

The Jap's body is gone, but his blood is still on the floor, covered in flies. When I walk by, they all buzz away. The sound is horrible. One gets in my ear, and I slap at it with my free hand. With the other, I drag the last bag of weed and leave it next to the freezer. The smell of iron and gunpowder mixes with the smell of marijuana. I dry the sweat off my face with the sleeve of my T-shirt. In front of me is a wall of marijuana bricks.

That's it, I tell myself.

That's it.

Gamarra wipes his beard with a towel and Centurión opens one of the gifts we stole.

"Funstation?" he says, taking out a video game system. "What the hell is this? Felipe's not missing out on anything." He tosses it away. "I hope the other stuff's better."

"Take a look," says Gamarra. He puts the towel on the

back of a chair and hands him a brick and a bud. Centurión smells it like a girl who's been given a flower.

"Beautiful." He puts it in his pocket and motions for us to sit.

On top of the table is beer, *pan dulce*, and Mantecol.

Gamarra sits down to his boss's right. I sit on the other side. I shake my T-shirt to unstick it from my skin. Cerro Porteño and Flamengo went to drown their sorrows over Tagui between some princesses' legs. As soon as we finished unloading the bricks, Alvarenga disappeared without a word. Centurión cuts himself a slice of *pan dulce* and shoves it in his mouth.

"Did Tagui's shotgun make it?" he asks. Gamarra nods. "Good. Tagui had shit for brains. He watched too many of those new action movies. Steven Seagal syndrome. Go over to his house and he'd have *Under Siege* posters on the wall, 1 and 2."

Centurión cranes his neck and smells the bud again.

"And how did our friend here do?"

"For a fag, Little Cruz did okay."

Centurión stretches a black thong in his hands like a rubber band.

"You think he's ready?"

"I think he better be."

"What are you talking about?" I ask.

Centurión keeps playing with the black thong. The lace strains. He crumples it and brings it to his nose.

"There's no two ways about it. Whiskey and women have the best aroma when they're between twelve and eighteen years old."

Gamarra chokes on his Mantecol and spews a few pieces onto the table.

"Do you want to tell me what you're talking about?"

"The other part of your job."

"Listen, Centurión. My brother lost fifty kilos of weed. With all the bricks we brought back, you can build yourself a house."

"I can build myself a whole neighborhood once I've sold them, but piled up like that they aren't worth shit. You came here to finish your brother's work, and when they got him, he wasn't on vacation."

I point at him. My index finger is shaking.

"You got back what he lost. Well done, A-plus. Now you've got to get it across."

I shake my head, drop my arm, and grip the back of the chair. Sherman comes in the green door. He's wearing a kitchen apron and a welder's mask. He bends down and gropes for a few gas cans in a corner.

"Gamarra," he says, "leave the tank full next time."

"You know how it is, you get going and you can't stop."

Sherman grabs a half-full can and when he turns to open the door, I see that he's naked. Centurión pinches off another piece of *pan dulce* with his fingers.

"That girl a few minutes ago thought she could say no,

too. Waste of time for her and for me. When you do things the hard way, it all ends in blood. I fucked her so hard she left my dick looking like a tube of lipstick. If you tell me no, you'll make out worse than she did."

Behind the door, I can hear a car engine start, then a chain saw.

"Or maybe I'll put you right out of your misery. Sherman there learned a few things from your old man. As soon as he started hanging around, he'd come and tell me the stories he heard at the bars. One time they said Samuel put so much voltage through a guy, he left the whole city without electricity. Sherman loved all that shit. And we weren't exactly choir boys, you know? If he'd paid that much attention at university, he'd be figuring out the universe like that Hawking guy in the wheelchair, instead of putting people in wheelchairs."

The sound of the chain saw is muffled as it bites into meat. Cutting. Cutting again. Bumps. Things falling. The plastic tablecloth sticks to my hands. My fingers leave dirty prints.

"Just get it across?" I say, gritting my teeth.

Centurión finishes his glass of beer.

"You tell me how you want to end up in the Paraná. In a boat or in a bag."

I stand up so fast I knock the chair over. Centurión's right hand jumps to the Smith & Wesson. Gamarra's already pointing his Beretta at me. I put my hands up.

"Boat," I say. Centurión smiles and nods at Gamarra,

who puts his pistol away. He takes another piece of Mantecol.

"So?" I ask. "What are you waiting for?"

"Take it easy, champ. I'm not going to make you work
today, it's Christmas."

With a slam of the door, Sherman comes back in. Instead
of the welder's mask, he's wearing Mateo Docabo's cap.
Blood drips from his apron.

"He looks like a maxipad," says Gamarra.

"Suck my balls."

"Don't you mean your ovaries?"

"If you want, you can do it yourself next time."

"It's boring when they're dead. If you don't like it, go cry
to your daddy."

"Same old shit," Centurión says and looks at me. "Everybody likes to cook, but nobody wants to do the dishes."
When I don't return his smile, he adds, "You can go now,
kid. Rest those arms, you'll need them tomorrow. Get some
ass, it's on the house."

Sherman wrings out the apron, and a spurt of blood
splashes to the floor. Centurión smells the bud in his pocket
again before putting the thong back against his face.

"And you, Gamarra," he says, "go get me Docabo's other
daughter. We'll see if it goes better."

He winks an eye at me, and I leave. The hallway is like
a sauna. I feel dizzy. I take two steps, then grab my head.
My hand touches the wall and slips on the damp surface. I

stop. The music rises; I can't understand the words. A high-pitched sound gets louder with each step I take. My ears are exploding. I close my eyes. I slam my fist against the wall. I punch it again, and the plaster cracks under my knuckles. One more punch. I open the door. I run into the guy with the salmon pink shirt and the Uzi. He's probably telling me I'm a piece of shit, but I'm not listening. I run into someone else. His cap falls off his head and bills fall from his hand. They land on the stage. A Sleeping Beauty rushes to pick them up. The guy says something to me. He must be telling me I'm a piece of shit, too. He comes at me. He sees my face. He sees my hands, my knuckles covered in blood with bits of plaster stuck to them. He purses his lips, and turns his back on me. A Little Red Riding Hood dodges me. I sit down at the bar and order two beers. I attack the first one. As the beer disappears, the music starts to come together.

Only a few dads are left, along with some sons watching the princesses who have taken off their costumes and are walking around in thongs and bras. Alvarenga's nowhere to be seen. I finish off the can, crush it, and toss it away. I grab the second one and rest it against the back of my neck, then my knuckles. A brunette comes over, touches my hand, and smiles. She's got fewer teeth than a baby. Her bra is too small for her, and the black areolas of her nipples are showing.

"Want to see the rest, honey?" She pulls her thong down a little with her index finger.

"Thanks, but I'm a little short."

"I like small ones, too."

I rub my fingers together.

"Money."

"You don't need much *pirá piré* with me."

I shake my head. She shrugs and goes after a guy at the other end of the bar. Same bait: she takes his hand and pulls down her thong. He bites. I pop open my second beer. Flamengo and Cerro walk by with their arms around two girls. They see me and yell something in Guarani. The only thing I can pick out is *curuzú cuatiá* and I don't even know what the hell it means.

"Go fuck yourselves," I say. They walk off laughing.

I down the beer in two chugs. I go for a third can, but it isn't enough. Someone's talking from behind me.

"Antonio," I hear. Once. Twice. Three times before I realize they're talking to me. Cinderella. Still wearing her costume and runny makeup. "Are you okay?"

"Are you?"

I look at her tits. I wonder how she'll look once she's fully developed. She'll be pretty, as long as she doesn't stay here.

"Is this enough for all night?" I say and hold out a fan of bills.

She grabs the money first, then my hand. Her fingers are callused and sweaty.

"This way."

A line of red bulbs and moans in a patio surrounded by rooms. They put up a sun screen with fishing nets and torn lingerie. A chalkboard is hanging on one door: *Knock before entering* and below that *No blood in the rooms.*

"Go on in, I'll be right back," she says and opens the door to a room a little smaller than a prison cell.

I wonder if they've locked my brother up yet. Cinderella goes into a bathroom. Before she closes the door, I can see a washbasin on the floor.

In the room, on top of a dresser with a plastic tablecloth on top, are creams and shampoos. A holy card of San Cayetano. "Peace, bread, and work." A clothesline hangs between two walls. The rest of the space is grey and water-stained. Instead of a bed, there's an ironing board on the floor. I lie down. Cinderella comes back. Her hair is wet and sticks to her neck. She takes off her dress. Her thong looks more like a moth-eaten lace than lingerie. She takes off her bra, and I see that her nipples barely stand out on her skin.

"Stop," I say.

"What's wrong?"

I shake my head.

"You don't have to do that."

"Do you want me to . . . ?" She touches her mouth with her hand.

"No." I push my body against the wall and pat the ironing board. "I just need a place to rest."

She looks at me. Her thin eyebrows arch.

"Come on. You need a rest, too."

She shrugs and puts her bra back on. She lies down next

to me. We stare at the ceiling. The board is so small that half of her body won't fit. She rolls onto her side and looks at me. This close up, she looks even younger.

"How did you end up here?" she says. "You seem like you're nothing like these people."

"Brown eyes and this nose aren't the only things I got from my old man."

She lifts up my shirt. I raise my arms, and she pulls it all the way off. She stands up, and when she hangs it on the line, I get a good view of her ass. I take out the Colt and my knife and hide them between my hip and the wall.

"I never knew mine," she says and lies down on her side, using her hands as a pillow. "My mom, either. And I lived with her for ten years. I can only remember little things. Like that her hair was always shiny. That she got up when me and my sister were going to bed. She said the light hurt her eyes. Laura knew her, though. She's seven years older than me. When I asked her what Mom was like, she said, "Mom was Camba Bolsa, Ani." When she realizes she's let her name slip, she pouts her lips. "Camba Bolsa is a story moms from here use to get their kids to go to sleep. He's a man who puts little kids in his bag and then leaves them alone in the middle of the jungle. My sister was right. Our mom was always dirty and carrying a baggie or two, more if she had some money. And she ended up leaving us alone."

She smiles sadly. She reaches out and wipes a line of

mud off me with her finger. My chest is so tight my ribs are sticking out. I swallow.

"You're here because of your mother?" I ask. My jaw crunches.

She shakes her head and then rests it against my chest.

"Once we were on our own, we'd go and work in the *yerba mate* plantations every May. You can tell, right?" She shows me the calluses on one hand. "We slept in a tent, and a few times we had to spend everything we earned on medicine. Laura had bad lungs. Ña Betty, a medicine woman who worked with us, said she wouldn't last long. In April, my sister told me we didn't have to go there again. We moved to Posadas, to a really big house with a bathroom. We had a room each and even a TV. She'd gotten work outside the city, taking care of a baby for a family in Buenos Aires. She'd go for a few days at a time. Then a few weeks ago she left, but she never came back. A little while after that, there was a knock on the door and that guy with the beard was there. He said my sister had disappeared and owed them money." Her voice breaks and she has to cough before she can go on. "I told them to take the TV and the VCR. They said she owed them a little more than that."

Her eyes close. She can't be more than sixteen, and she's already a woman. I'm almost thirty and I'm still a kid. I hug her. My chest gets wet. I don't know if it's her damp hair or her tears, and I don't ask. I hold her a little longer.

"Nice story, huh?" she says. Her lips appear between the locks of hair falling across her face. "Tell me a nicer one."

Once upon a time, my brother crossing the Paraná, my niece unwrapping a bullet for Christmas, a grandfather and his son and a Colt putting holes in their bodies.

"Let's just go to sleep," I say and start to pull my arm away.

"No," she says. "Leave it there." I hug her again. "Thanks, Antonio."

"Sleep well, Ani."

"Anyelén," she says with a smile.

She makes her head comfortable on my chest. The adrenaline starts to fade away, my head drifts like it's floating on a tide, moans and shouts, voices underwater.

A buzzing sound wakes me up. I open my eyes. I scratch my ear, and a mosquito flies away. I blink. My eyes are burning. Everything's blurry. I have to blink a few more times. It takes me a minute to realize where I am. The sweaty sheets sticking to me like cling wrap. Anyelén isn't here. I open the door. It's still nighttime, and red twenty-watt stars glow on the patio. A girl goes into a room in front of mine with two guys. The door next to that opens and out comes a man so fat he has to turn sideways to squeeze through. Coming out behind him is Anyelén. She walks over with her eyes on the floor. She comes into the room, puts a few bills into a shampoo bottle, and goes back out. Only then does she look at me.

"I have to work off my debt."

She straightens her dress and presses out the wrinkles on her stomach with her hand.

"Are you . . . are you free? Honey?" mumbles a drunk.

"Of course, sweetheart." She motions for him to go into the next room down.

I lie in the bed. Anyelén's moans mingle with the man's grunts. I think about Alina, trapped here, about Lelé being scavenged. About someone breaking them open, taking a piece of them with each orgasm they splatter on their skin. I think about all these women whose only damp parts are their eyes. About cries for help disguised as dirty talk, desperate screams disguised as moans. If an alarm existed to announce the end of the world, it would sound exactly like those screams.

Maybe this is it, the announcement. Maybe it's just an echo.

I put on my shirt, grab the Colt and the knife, and go back into the bar. There's no more music or dancing. A few people asleep, others passed out on the tables with their unfinished beers in their hands. Half an hour later, I join their ranks.

A backlit silhouette wakes me up. It takes me a minute to figure out who the hell it is.

"Morning, princess," says Gamarra with a steaming cup of coffee in his hand. "I hope you got some nice beauty sleep. You've got a long day ahead of you."

I rub my face. The sunlight bouncing off the patio hurts my eyes. I don't see Alvarenga or her. It doesn't matter. You learn to do your time alone.

"If it's going to be such a long one, we might as well get started," I say. "Let's go."

# 17.

The reflection of the lamp shimmers on the Paraná like a flame.

I throw a stone and shatter it. With all the others I've thrown in while I've been waiting, it won't be long before they break the surface like the top of a mountain.

Next to an improvised dock made of tree trunks, the boughs of the willows scratch the river. Farther down, the branches seem to push three boats that bob in the wind.

Behind me, higher up the bank, three wooden houses painted moss green are visible between the trees. In the door of the closest one, Centurión stands smoking a cigarette. A Ranger with tinted windows is parked where the white Isuzu was a few hours ago. It hasn't come back yet. A guy in a beret heads for the dock with two pieces of wood as big around as lampposts under his arms.

I throw another stone.

A guy walks in front of me and leaves a sack on the boat.

A few bricks of coke fall out. The man passes by me. His eyebrows look like two fuzzy cats. He goes up the bank and disappears behind the Ranger. Centurión flicks the cigarette butt away and goes inside the cabin. The guy in the beret balances a plank on top of a piece of wood and gets to work with his machete.

The reflection of the trees in the river breaks up completely. The guy with the eyebrows goes by again and loads another twenty kilos in the boat, which is moving less and less with all the weight.

The last time I rowed a boat was when we went fishing as kids. Samuel would give us rods and a couple of worms, then make himself comfortable on the shore with his *bota* bag and drink wine until he passed out. That was at least fifteen years ago. Rowing is like riding a bike, I tell myself and throw another rock.

Eyebrows walks by again. This time he's got a sack over each shoulder. The drops running down his face look more like sap than sweat.

The wind is blowing. The willows sink in the water, and the waves break against a rusted car on the shore. The smell of wet earth predicts rain. I can't see the shore on the Argentine side. Clouds of fog rest on the surface of the river as if the Paraná were a brownish sky.

The little lamps that hang from the other two cabins come on, and now there are three flames that mirror each other. Three candles, a shrine, and just like at the police station, the urge to pray, to believe in something, explodes in my chest.

The guy in the beret keeps hacking away with his machete, and the wood starts to take the shape of an oar. This time Eyebrows walks past with another guy whose shadow is so huge, I thought he was two people. He puts down a huge bag like the ones used for *yerba mate*. I've lost count of how many kilos he's loaded. The wind keeps blowing, but the boat doesn't even move. The full moon paints everything with a white halo, making the whole scene look like something from a dream.

Two halves of an oar broken in the middle come sailing through the air by my head.

"Sorry for the delay," says Centurión, shaking his hands. He digs at his skin with his nail and pulls a splinter from his palm. "Another problem with a rower."

I stand up and brush the dirt from my jeans. I stick the knife in my waistband and look at him.

"Looks like a storm's coming," he says.

"Then tell them to hurry up."

He lights another cigarette. He takes a drag and exhales the smoke. The shadows deepen the wrinkles on his face. He has a drop of blood on his neck, but no cuts.

"You know what it's like, Cruz. Fuck-ups don't last long here." He takes out a handkerchief and wipes his neck. "You'll have a little more trouble because of the holidays. We use fireworks to mark the route for the rowers, but as you can imagine, that's not much good this time of year. Let's hope you've got good instincts." He takes another drag on the cigarette and walks closer to me. "You're going to make two stops. The first one as soon as you cross. You're going to go along the shore until you see flashing lights. You stop there and drop off the first package. Are you getting this?"

I nod. A jab of pain goes up my arm and into my back.

"Then you're going to keep going until you come to the Garuhapé stream. You'll see a beach, and next to an altar to Gauchito Gil, there's a little path we made. Head in there along the river until you come to Route 12. When you get there, go straight until you see a house with the white Isuzu parked out front."

"And that's it?"

Centurión exhales smoke and taps off some ash.

"Your sister-in-law should go see a shrink," he says. "Gamarra told me she's still got the same clothes on. She can't take care of a little girl like that."

"My family's my problem."

"Well, there's one thing we agree on."

Eyebrows and the Giant leave another bunch of sacks in the boat. It's barely staying afloat.

"One more bag and that thing's going to sink," I say. "Faith might move mountains, but my arms can't."

"So have some fucking faith."

Giant raises his arm, and Centurión drops his right hand like a checkered flag.

"Don't worry, you won't be taking that much."

Eyebrows sits in the open space between the bags and starts rowing. I let out a breath. My chest shrinks by half.

"Come on," Centurión says, starting up the bank.

When we get to the cabin, our skin turns orange in the dim light of the lamp. Centurión flicks his cigarette butt away. Inside I hear noises I can't identify.

"In the business world today, kid," he says, "you've got to stay one step ahead. You've got to think about renewable energy. Wind and solar and all that shit are way off the mark. With weed, you sell it, they smoke it, and it's gone. A hole's got no shelf life, Cruz. *Three* holes, now? Forget it." He opens the door. "Meet your package."

In one corner are two girls gagged and tied together with ropes. Their T-shirts are too big and their shorts are too short. One lifts her head and looks at me: it's Docabo's youngest daughter.

"What the fuck is this?"

"Renewable energy."

"Forget it, Centurión."

"Don't think about these girls. Think about yours."

He shows me the Smith & Wesson stuck into his pants.

"Anyway, don't worry about them. They're never going to be out of work. They've got their futures all figured out. You don't." Docabo's daughter scrunches her eyebrows together and starts to cry. The rag in her mouth muffles her sobs. "Things used to be easier, Cruz. You took them across the bridge, and that was it. But a while back we had a problem with one of them raising hell at the border. Minors need guardians, and getting into fake IDs is a pain in the ass. I'll leave that to other people. Outsourcing, that's the other key to economics."

I feel like throwing up. The boat starts to disappear in the mist over the Paraná. I steady myself against the wall to keep from falling.

"And the worst thing is people say I'm working in the white slave trade."

"You're fucking sick."

"What's sick is saying these girls are white. You'd have to be colorblind. Did you see these girls? White? I've taken shits whiter than these two. And just wait, I haven't shown you the best part yet. The third concept of economics. Utilization. Come here."

He never turns his back to me. I take my hands off the Colt. I think about Lelé and Viviana. About Alina. The Docabo girl sways, doped out of her mind. The other girl has passed out completely.

"If they said I was trafficking black girls, I could take that, but there's no reasoning with people." We go into a narrow hallway. I can hear a fan and a generator. To our right is a door. Centurión turns the knob. "So as you can see, we had to utilize those holes and give them something to make them white."

He opens the door and walks inside. Anyelén is kneeling

over some diary papers. A strong gust coming from the fan blows her hair over her face. A couple of strands catch on her mouth, shiny with saliva or something that looks like it. Centurión removes them, his fingers leaving a red mark on her face.

"I told that asshole to put her hair up, but he always has his headphones on." He points to Sherman, whose back is to me as he plays air drums over by the portable scale.

Centurión grabs something from the table, but I can't see what it is because his body is obstructing my view. I take a step toward the side to get a better a view.

"Open your mouth, baby," he says. "Body of Christ."

And he shoves a condom full of drugs in Anyelén, who lifts her neck, coughs, spits it out, and topples to the ground. Centurión *tsks* and picks it up, now covered in dirt. He spits on it and wipes it off on his shirt.

"Come on, baby. I know you swallow much bigger things for breakfast."

He tries again. The condom enters her mouth, her throat pulses forcefully, as if her heart was there. She squeezes her eyes shut, gathers strength, and swallows it.

My body buckles and I have to lean against the wall. Spread across the table are a mountain of condoms full of liquid coke, waiting.

"Fill her up, kid."

Sherman removes his headphones and takes his father's place.

Anyelén opens her eyes and sees me. She watches me as if her words are in her eyes and not on her lips, as if her mouth is anything but a mouth. She shuts her eyes and I feel the silence of her gaze. I will carry that silence forever like a tattoo.

Centurión pulls the door closed, leaving it open a crack, and I look away.

"I'm doing you a favor, kid. Your brother lost almost fifty kilos, and you're only going to have to cross with three. The two girls in there are the first package, and this little lady is the second one."

I need air. I go running outside. My body lurches forward, but I can't throw up. My eyes sting with sweat. Centurión rests his hand on my shoulder.

"The saddest part of the whole thing is that this is the first time a lot of them have ever used a condom. The girl passed out in there, she's fifteen and already had two abortions. What kind of person is that?"

I shove him away from me, and he falls ass-first to the ground. He turns to face me. I touch the Colt. My fingers close around the grip. Centurión leans toward me, hands open, encouraging me to shoot him.

"If you take your piece out, kid, you better fucking use it."

I squeeze the gun. I take a breath. He pounds his chest twice. I take my hand off the gun and he smiles.

"That's better." He gets up. "If you want to go after who's guilty here, talk to your brother."

The boats look like two dry leaves dragged along by the

wind. The guy in the beret is gone, but there are two freshly carved oars on the dock.

"They're ready to go," says Sherman as he comes outside, pulling off his rubber gloves.

"Bring them out."

I turn and walk down to the river. Sherman comes down with the first two girls, who can barely walk. His father appears behind him, pushing Anyelén along with his hand on the back of her neck. She's also gagged and has her hands cuffed behind her back. She walks by me with her head down. Sherman already put the other two girls in the middle and tied another set of hooks to a hole in the wood. Centurión sits Anyelén down at the other end.

"Get a move on," he says and hands me a set of keys. "Gamarra's going to be waiting for the little one. She's got a photo shoot and a flight to Spain. If you haven't left her with him in three hours, he's going to have to find himself another little mule. He's already got his eye on one."

I put one foot in the boat and almost fall, I'm trembling so much.

"Take it easy," says Centurión. "When this is over, we'll find out whether you're a Cruz, or just a cross in a cemetery." He hands me the oars.

The girls look at me. The waves make a hollow sound as they slap against the boats. The fog on the other sides looks more and more like clouds.

I start to row.

# 18.

The wake of the boat is a scar that extends across the river.

We move along parallel to the Argentine shore. The bank is a wall of trees. Anyelén looks at the mist behind us. The other girls sit with their heads leaning against each other, and the Docabo girl's black hair mixes with the other girl's blonde highlights like the pelt of a jaguar.

I hear the oars beating the water and the chirping of all kinds of animals. I hold my right arm still and keep rowing with the left to straighten the boat out. I dodge a few branches that stick out of the water. The clouds are lines that stretch out against the sky. The wind makes them flow like rivers that come together and then separate.

I row.

I row to escape that brownish sky.

I row to reach land.

Anyelén's hair falls across her forehead. She twists her

neck and tries to shake it off. She whips her head to the side. Her body bends in half with each shake. I imagine the condoms squeezing against each other in her stomach. Her bangs move but end up covering her face again. I want to tuck them behind her ear. I want to hold her, stuff her full of laxatives and get all that shit out of her. I want to give that bullet back to Gamarra. I want to put a kilo of lead inside Centurión.

All I can do is row.

The Docabo girl's head bobs like a reed. She tries to open her eyes. Her eyelashes flutter. They look like two dragonflies crushed against a windshield while trying to escape. The other girl's chin is against her chest, and she's breathing through her mouth.

A circle of yellow bursts on the water, and then hits my face. I bring up my forearm to shield myself. The ray of a flashlight hidden in the vegetation. A piece of plant falls into the river and bounces against the boat. A branch comes loose, and a man with a machete appears. He waves at me to come closer. A guy standing next to him has a shotgun against his shoulder. The prow of the boat hits the ground between them.

"You're late, *chamigo*," says the one holding the machete.

I get out. A spider crawls across a leaf in front of my face. I reach into my pocket. Under my wallet I find the keys. I hand them to him.

"Tell Don Centurión not to send them so drugged up next

time," says the guy with the shotgun while his friend takes off their handcuffs. "It's fine this time because they're so little, but you don't even know what it's like carrying them through the jungle. It's like they're filling them up with bricks instead of coke."

"Take them, Juárez," says the other one.

The guy with the shotgun reaches out and grabs the brunette. She slips, and they both end up face-down in the mud.

"Goddamn it," says Juarez. "I'm telling you. We've got to walk two miles with them like this. We're going to have to carry them. And to top it all off, the wife wants me to cut back the weeds when I get back."

"We do the heavy lifting. And they go to Europe."

"Are you done?" I ask.

"The other guy was cooler. What happened to him?"

"I don't know. I don't care."

The guy with the shotgun picks the two girls up. They're shaking. Their knees knock into each other. The brunette grabs her stomach like a pregnant woman. They take one step and fall again.

"For fuck's sake," says the guy with the shotgun.

"Juárez, can you cut the shit? The boss is going to give me hell because the forger will waste two hours putting makeup on them for the IDs, and he'll end up charging him a fortune. If he pays me any less, it's coming out of your cut."

"Take it easy, Nika, if I want someone to bust my balls I've got my wife."

"Are you guys just about done?" I ask.

The one with the machete rubs Anyelén's knee, and she jerks it away.

"Too bad you're not leaving us this one," he says. He steps off the boat and gives me back the keys. "Next time I hope they don't send us another prick like you." He wipes his hands. "Come on, Juárez, give them to me."

He grabs the girls and pulls on the rope to get them up. I get in the boat and take the oars. Juárez has one of his boots resting on the prow.

"And a merry fucking Christmas," he says and pushes the boat off. "Porteños . . . These city assholes, no manners."

I turn the boat, rowing with just my left hand to get it back parallel with the shore. The two guys disappear into the vegetation, and I start rowing with both arms. A blue firework cuts through the sky. Anyelén follows it with her eyes while I watch its reflection in the Paraná. It explodes. There's a cascade, and then it's gone.

Anyelén tosses her head to get the hair out of her face. Cinderella after midnight. Without the makeup and tight clothes, she's not even the shadow of a woman. She tries to say something, but the words are lost in her gag. I reach out and pull it off. And then I put her hair behind her ear.

"You can take these off, too." She nods at the cuffs. "I'm not going to run away." I hesitate. I shake my head. I keep rowing. "I chose this," she insists. "I'm not going anywhere."

I put my hand in my pocket and find the key. It takes me three tries to get it in. I take the cuffs off her.

"How the hell did you choose this?"

"The other stuff wasn't much better," she says, massaging her wrists. "I want to find my sister and I needed them to let me go fast. That guy with the beard showed up this morning and said there were two ways for me to work off the debt and that it depended on what I wanted to swallow: a kilo of coke or a thousand of cum."

"Don't say anything and just stay calm. Everything's going to be fine."

"You stay calm."

I squeeze the freshly hewn oar and feel the splinters biting into my hand.

"When you get to Europe," I say, "don't come back. Run away."

"You're not listening to me. I want to find Laura. She didn't come back, and that means something must have happened to her."

"They'll get you again if you come back."

"She took care of me my whole life."

"Couldn't it just be that your sister took off?"

"She wouldn't leave me alone."

"Okay," I say. "Just calm down. Don't talk."

"I am calm. The silence makes me nervous, all those animal noises."

"Okay, then talk."

She looks at her hands. She scratches her neck, fingering a chain that disappears inside her T-shirt.

"When Lau turned fifteen, our mom gave her a ring. It was pretty. It was silver and it had her initials in gold: LF," she says, touching her ring finger. "I remember the F looked kind of weird. It had a tail at the bottom, too. Like it used to be an E, and they cut the bottom off. Mom said it has been made for her, and we believed her. We were really stupid." She smiles at me.

I look over my shoulder, but there's no sign of the stream. My T-shirt is solid water stuck to my skin. We hit a couple of little lilypads that bend against the front of the boat like wet newspaper. She grabs them and throws them to the side. She watches them as we leave them behind.

"Back then my sister used to work in a bakery. She had to knead the dough, so she left the ring at home every morning. One afternoon she came back and it wasn't there. Branches." I frown at her, and she points over my shoulder.

I stop rowing with my right arm and move the left oar. A couple of branches break against the boat, but I avoid the biggest ones.

"The day the ring disappeared, my mom was snorting all night and all morning. She and my sister had a big fight. I told her not to be sad, and she said the only thing she was sorry about was that Mom had cut off the bottom of the E. If it was still there, maybe it would have been enough for her to die of an overdose. After that, my mom took off."

A few more lilypads that are stuck to the front of the boat come loose and get caught in the oars. I shake them until they come off.

"With everything I swallowed," says Anyelén, holding her stomach, "I'm sure my mom would love me now. At least until they take it out."

She puts her hand into the river.

"I heard that they have us travel with other women. A family is less suspicious and they can take more. There's no way the mother they give me could be worse than my real one."

This is all a sickness, I tell myself. She takes her hand out of the water and wipes it on her T-shirt. A bolt of lightning cuts across the sky behind her. Where the hell is that stream?

"When I turned fifteen," she says, trying to bury a silence that seems to crush her, "Laura said she had to take a trip. Ever since we moved, I hadn't met almost anyone. I hadn't signed up for school. The only people I knew were from the German Club where we went to skate. One of the girls came to pick me up on my birthday, and we went to the Club. They threw a surprise party for me. And my sister was there." She puts her hand into her T-shirt and pulls out a chain. "She gave me this. It's beautiful. With my initials engraved on the back. But it's nothing compared to having her with me."

I wonder where she finds the strength to form the smile that fills half her face. She lets it fall apart and says:

"If there's anyone who knows what having a sibling means, it's you, Tomás."

The chirps disappear. A bird flies by and disappears into the jungle. Silence. I row more slowly. There's something strange that grows, like the sound of a bomb about to fall. And it explodes.

Tomás.

"You're not Antonio," she says. "I know your name is Tomás. Tomás Cruz. And that you're not here because of your dad. You're here because your brother Sebastián is in jail." She pauses. "And I know he's in jail because they sold him out."

The sound of the oars disappears.

"What are you talking about? How do you know all that?"

"They forget about all the holes in us they don't use, and that I understand more than they think." She touches her ears. "They started talking to each other in Guarani . . ."

"Who? Who did you hear?"

"That kid, the young one with the big nose. And the other one with crooked teeth. The ones who were with you the other day. They had soccer jerseys with black and red stripes . . ."

Flamengo and Cerro Porteño.

"I know who you mean. What did they tell you?"

"They didn't tell me anything. But I heard that their boss had your brother put away. He gave him up to the police

because your brother was working with another man . . ."
She thinks. "He had a weird name. Del Piero or something
like that."

"Di Pietro," I spit.

She nods. I want to grab my head, but I'm holding the
oars.

"They gave him up to the police. And they said that . . ."

"That what?"

A bird flies to another tree. I duck my head down. She
bites her lips.

"I couldn't really understand. They said something about
jail, and visits, and that history repeats itself. Tradition or
something."

One of the oars slips out of my hand and I rush to grab
it. The water breaking against the sides. Another flash of
lightning.

"I shouldn't have said anything," she says.

"You did the right thing. Everything's going to be fine."

"Tomás. Calm down."

I take a break. I let the air out. I row. My arms are
cramping up. Something falls on my head. A drop makes a
circle in the water, then another falls.

"Tomás."

"I know. It's raining."

She shakes her head and points behind me. A hundred
yards farther down, the jungle falls back and the stream
appears. I row with all the strength I have left, but I feel like

we're anchored. The rain picks up speed. More drops, circles that merge with others, links in a chain. I'm shackled to the Paraná. I row. I try to break free. The current starts to suck me to one side. I don't bother to dodge some branches. They break. There's a buzzing. With my elbow, I try to scare off a mosquito, but the sound gets louder. It's not a mosquito. A yellow spot in the river moves closer. I follow the ray of light like the fuse on a bomb until I see the Border Patrol boat that appears in front of us.

Anyelén gasps. Land is about ten yards above our heads up the sheer face of the bank, and there's no clearing for us to get out. The river flows on. If I turn, I might be able to make it. The beam of light stretches out and turns toward the vegetation, lighting up the altar to Gauchito Gil. The bank ends in a beach. I could turn and go downstream with the current or get out there. The boat comes closer, slowly. There are two officers on the deck with bullet-proof vests and camo uniforms.

"Get us out of here, Tomás. Please."

"Calm down."

The shore breaks up and curves when we move into the stream. I turn and point the prow at the opposite shore. Anyelén's fingers dig into my arm. The shore is right there. It looks closer and closer. Until it disappears. I'm blind. The lamp shines right in my eyes.

"Stop!"

When we bump into the shore, I lurch forward and knock

my forehead on the edge of the boat. I open my eyes. The blindness disappears. Anyelén yanks me to my feet.

"Let's go, let's go," she says and starts up the bank. Ten yards farther in, it becomes jungle. We plunge into the darkness. The moonlight that filters through is our only guide.

"Stay where you are," says the other officer and fires a shot into the air.

The animals hidden in the branches all start to croak at once and disorient us. A branch snaps. I turn around. The Border Patrol boat runs into ours and breaks it apart. Four men in uniform get out. Something comes flying at me and hits my ear. I bring my arms up to protect myself. Anyelén is ahead of me, and I try to follow her. The beams of the officers' flashlights cross over each other. Someone fires a shot. This time it's not into the air. Anyelén trips, but before she falls, I catch her. I ask her if she's okay, and she says yes. The flashlights split up, two toward us and two in another direction. After a moment, the jungle disappears: the path Centurión told me about. I motion to Anyelén and we move inland. I keep one hand on her waist and the other on the Colt. There are so many plants that the flashlight beams are cut into a thousand pieces and look like a line of fireflies.

"Wait a minute," she says and stops, resting her hands on her knees.

My chest is bursting. I think about her stomach and rub her back.

"Come on," I say.

The path is too long. I can't see where it ends. There are parts that are so dense the moonlight can't even filter through, and we fumble our way forward through the trees. The rain barely gets through.

"Don't let them catch us."

"Everything's okay."

The flashlights behind us, the breath of a wild beast with nine-millimeter fangs. Our walk becomes a trot, and we speed up even more when we hear a shot close by. Layers of spiderwebs piled on top of each other strangle the trees and everything under them. We run until Anyelén trips and falls face first to the ground. I'm not fast enough to catch her. I see her stomach bounce off the ground. She rolls over and grabs her foot.

"Let me see," I say. I move her foot until I find a sliver of light. She has a cut above her ankle. I wipe it off with my shirt, but more bloods comes out. "It's nothing."

I help her up, but as soon as she puts weight on her foot, her ankle gives out.

"I can't," she says. "I can't."

I put her down and squat down next to her.

"Grab on." I hold my arms out to pick her up. She puts her arms around my neck, then I grab her legs and stand up. "Hang on tight. Don't let go."

She's heavy. Too heavy. With the little strength I have left and how scared I am, her hundred and ten pounds feel like a ton. Her fingers are clutched together on my chest. The flashlights are still close.

There's another shot. They yell something at us, but the only thing I can hear are her words in my ear. "Let's go. Let's go. Please." The blood dripping from her foot makes me slip. I stop for a second, dry it off, and keep going. She mumbles in my ear.

"The wings of the *panambí* dance in the voice of Anahí."

"What's wrong?" I ask and slow down. She doesn't answer, just keeps singing.

"*Panambí* petal wings, *che raperame, reseva rejerok. Nde pepo kuarahy'ame.*"

I turn around. Her eyes dance, lost. I lean her against a tree and move her so that a ray of moonlight falls on her face. I grab her head and shake it. I try to open her eyelids, but her eyes won't focus.

"Ani. Talk to me."

"*Panambí*, in the shadow of your red petal wings . . ."

The smile on her lips is deformed by a cough, then a croak, and choking. She's white. Deathly white. Her chest spasms. Her hands tremble and fall to the ground. Her head drags across the trunk, and her hair falls across her face. I touch her neck, her chin, her cheeks. The silence of her blood on my fingertips.

I shake my head. Once. Twice. My knees sink into the earth. I put my hands over my mouth.

The beams of light start to come closer and become bars.

I wipe my face with my shirt. I pull it off and lay it out on the ground. I think about Seba. And above all, I think about my niece and Alina.

I slam my hands against the ground. I hit the earth until my hands hurt so much they fall asleep, until they're no longer my hands. A thread of saliva comes out of her mouth. I lay her down on the ground. Her hair falls across her face, and I tuck it behind her ears one last time and close her eyelids. I reach under her to take the chain from her neck and put it in my pocket.

I lift up Anyelén's T-shirt and cover her face. I take out my old man's knife. The cross on the handle is the only one she'll have.

"I'm sorry," I say, and plunge the blade into her stomach.

I dig around. I open her. I cut. I find what I'm looking for. I pull it out and put it on my shirt. The condoms full of coke squeeze and stretch the walls of her stomach. I cut a hole and they come sliding out one after the other, slithering like worms. One is burst and wrinkled. I grab it. I take a couple of steps and throw it far away from her. Then I throw up. My chest caves in and my hands rest on my knees, which hold out for a few seconds then hit the ground. I throw up everything I have left inside me.

I stand up as best I can. I'm dizzy. A beam of light hits a tree trunk in front of me, and the yellow spot starts to shrink as it gets closer. I go back over to her and bend down. I pull down her T-shirt. Stains start to appear above the two cuts in her stomach. Two red petal wings opening.

I tie a knot in the shirt and close it like a bag so nothing falls out.

And I run.

Until I lose her.

Until I lose their shouts and their beams of light.

Until I lose everything I am.

# 19.

The only remnant of the storm is the wind.

A set of Christmas lights hangs from the roof of a house and reflect off the white Isuzu. Leaves pile up on the windshield. Through the windows, I can see a shed farther back. A shadow appears through the curtain, and a few seconds later, the door opens. Gamarra looks at me and swivels his neck to look outside, left, right, until he sees the improvised bag made out of my T-shirt. He closes his eyes and starts to laugh as he opens the door the rest of the way.

"Looks like it was a tough one, Little Cruz."

He keeps laughing and walks through the room holding his stomach. He chokes and coughs. A guy with horn-rimmed glasses and sideburns turns his head to look me up and down. He pushes his glasses up the bridge of his nose and goes back to working on a laptop sitting in front of him. On the table are ink, printers, stamps, and some other things I can't even recognize. I sidestep a camera on a tripod pointed toward a light blue cloth hung on the wall and leave the bag next to the computer.

"What are you doing?" the guy says, covering his nose. "That thing smells like shit. Get it out of here."

Gamarra can't stop laughing. He wipes away a tear with one hand and massages the grip of his Beretta with the other. He sighs and straightens up.

"Take it easy," he says and picks up the bag. One of the condoms falls out and bounces to the floor. He leans over and puts it back on the shirt. He lets out another laugh. "I hope this wasn't an expensive shirt." A bead of saliva shines on his beard. "But seriously, this stuff happens because those girls aren't used to using condoms."

"Can you get that shit out of here?" insists the guy at the computer.

"Calm the fuck down." Gamarra slaps the back of his head. His glasses fall onto the keyboard. "What's your boss's number?"

"Auto-dial two. And if you're going to call Paraguay, call collect. Or I'll send you the bill."

"Don't worry, Jew," says Gamarra. "And you, Little Cruz, you wait here." He disappears behind a folding door.

The guy scratches the back of his neck and goes back to working on his computer. He's retouching wedding pictures. He corrects redeye and ups the contrast. I stare at the blue cloth on the wall, trying to imagine Anyelén there waiting for the picture.

"You've got to diversify," the guy says. "People don't get married as much anymore, and when girls turn fifteen they're going on trips instead of having the big party."

"I don't give a shit about what you do," I say before he goes on.

I sit down on a stool. My jeans are stiff from the mud and the blood. The guy tries to hand me a cup of coffee. I won't take it, and he ends up drinking it himself. The steam clouds up his glasses. I can hear Gamarra's voice from the other room. My head is pounding, and the goose egg on my forehead doesn't have much to do with it.

"Do you like the name?" says the guy, handing me an ID with no picture. "Ivana. It was going to be my first daughter's name."

Gamarra comes back in, points his finger at me, and shoots. He blows away the imaginary smoke.

"The keys to the chicken coop," he says to the guy with the glasses, who reaches into his pocket and hands them over.

"Be careful when you open it and don't forget to close the door behind you. I don't want to go running after them in this mud."

"What's going on?" I ask, but they ignore me.

Gamarra goes outside, and through the window I see him walk toward the shed at the back. The ground is turning orange with the first rays of the sun. When he opens the door, I can see piles of hay and some cages. A girl with no shoes peeks out. Her hands are tied, and she's wearing a muscle shirt with a stretched-out neck that ends at the top of her underwear. Gamarra drags her behind him. They come inside. She's shaking and there's so much mud on her feet it looks like she's wearing boots. She looks at us quickly, then drops her eyes to the floor. She lifts her hands to cover her face, and because they're tied together it looks like she's praying. She probably is.

The photographer comes over, grabs her by the chin, and looks her over.

"Do you really think she looks like the 'mother'?"

"All these dark bitches look the same," says Gamarra. "Over there, *mami*," he says, shoving her against the blue cloth. The guy with glasses hands her a new shirt. As she puts it on, he turns on the camera and gets ready to take her picture.

"Smile, honey," Gamarra says. "Thanks to our friend here, you're going to get a new diet and a new country." She stares at her feet. "Smile, goddamn it!"

The girl flinches. She lifts her head.

"Your hair," says the photographer. "And fix your clothes. This is for a passport picture, not *Penthouse Paraguay*."

With two fingers, she puts her hair behind her ear and straightens the neck of the shirt. I hear the sound of the shutter clicking. Once. Twice. Three times.

"Now we're going to go meet your mom," Gamarra says. He opens the folding door. On the other side is a hallway, and when he turns on the light, a room appears at the end of it. I manage to see two girls handcuffed to a stove before they step in front of me.

"She looks like an Ivana, doesn't she?" says the photographer as he unscrews the camera from the tripod.

I'm too far gone to care. They sold out my brother, they sent me to rob and shoot a father and his son, they made me open up a little girl like a garbage bag, but the only thing I want to do is hang my head, go home, and know that my girls are going to be okay, that no one is going to take their picture and stuff them full of dope, that my family is going to be safe.

But even so, I can't keep from touching the grip of the Colt when Gamarra comes back in and smiles at me. His teeth peek out from under his black beard like bones in a nest of burnt straw.

"Is everybody happy now?" I say. "If you don't mind, I'm going to get the fuck out of here and you all can go on with your business."

"Hang on, Little Cruz."

"What more do you want? I already got back what my brother lost and carried it across."

"In case you didn't notice, you showed up a little light."

"There's one condom missing."

"There's one girl missing."

"What do you mean?"

"I mean I just saved your ass. Our friend's boss gave us one of his. Now we've got to replace her."

"Don't even think about it."

He strokes his beard a couple of times.

"You know it's not a good idea to act like that, Little Cruz. I know I don't have to repeat myself." He reaches into his pocket and gives me a piece of paper. "Tomorrow night at ten," he says, "you're going to bring a girl there. End of story."

Do whatever it takes to keep them safe. Family sucks big time, I think and take the piece of paper. He reaches over to the desk and gives me a couple of cards.

"A little help," he says, winking. "And try to get this one there in one piece."

**AS SOON AS I** get home, I put the Colt and the knife on the table and feel like I've shed a second skin. My whole body starts to shake. I almost break my neck trying to take off my pants. The shower steals away the dirt and blood. The red mud turns into rivers and flows down my arm like an open vein bleeding out, chunks that don't belong to me anymore because I'm no longer what I was, but I also don't know what I am. I stand there until there's no dirt or mud left.

I pass out in bed.

When I wake up, the alarm clock reads 20:18, and next to it a number 3 is blinking on the answering machine. I hit play.

My sister-in-law asking me what the hell is going on.

Alina wishing me a merry Christmas and saying that if I ever happen to think of showing up at her house to surprise her, not to bother because she went to the south to see her mother. The sarcasm disappears little by little until disappointment fills her voice.

The last one. Samuel. I erase it as soon as I hear his voice.

Jeans and a shirt. Sneakers and cologne. The Colt and the knife. I look in the mirror and practice and practice until I believe it. Until the "You're the girl I need" sounds believable. And then I go out to find her.


**THE BAR I WALK** into makes the Tanimbu look like a five-star establishment. A cloud of weed smoke, smog clinging to the ceiling. A girl with a bruised eye hands a beer to a guy with a bandaged hand. Another girl walks over from the bar, and what looks from far away like a line of ants on her arm turns out to be a line of names tattooed prison style. There are more people in there who have had abortions than finished high school. It's that kind of place, I tell myself, repeating it in my head for the tenth time. This is the right place.

"You look like your name is Lourdes," I say to a girl sitting in front of me. She's a bleach blonde with boobs so big they stretch out the words printed in English on her tank top, which I doubt she could read even if they were in Spanish.

"My friends call me Lulu," she says, playing with the straw of the second fernet with Coke I've bought for her. "It's not the first time somebody's told me I should be a model. I even did a job once. Underwear. But it never got printed. They didn't seem too professional."

"Don't worry, we're experienced. You know Ingrid Grudke? You must because I'm sure you get told all the time you really look like her."

She smiles and takes another sip through the straw. The fernet in the glass keeps disappearing. She takes a deep breath and her bra starts to show. The EVERYTHING YOU KNOW IS WRONG written on her shirt stretches so much it looks like it's about to rip.

"Yeah, I know who she is."

"It was our agency that brought her to Buenos Aires. You could be the next Ingrid."

"Do you really think so?"

I think about the future I'll be stealing from her. She looks like ten grams of coke get pumped through her bloodstream every week. A mare with a broken leg—she's suffering anyway. Lelé does have a future.

"Do you have a card or something?" she asks.

I reach into my pocket and hand her one of the cards Gamarra gave me. Marcos Benavídez Modeling Agency. The paper is varnished and decorated with stars. Smoke and mirrors.

"And how much would you pay me?"

"Well, as a ballpark . . ." My mind blanks. I try to think of a number. A thousand is too little. Ten thousand isn't believable. "Two thousand pesos for each fashion show."

She lifts her eyebrows and lets out a "wow" but then starts to share her head slowly, doubting. You got conned into letting some assholes take pictures of you naked without even realizing it, and now you don't want to hop on a bus for two thousand pesos? Who the hell are you? Definitely not Ingrid Grudke, honey. You're nobody. I want to pull out the Colt and drag her out of there at gunpoint. I want to shoot down anyone who gets in my way and tell Gamarra, "Here you go."

"Let's do it. When could I start?" she says, looking at me with excitement in her eyes. She shows me a smile full of crooked teeth, a smile I'm going to shatter. But not forever, because I'm a nobody, too. I'm definitely not the kind of asshole you need to be to do something like this, to lock up that smile and kill it with drugs and desperate cocks. Centurión is a real piece of shit. And I'd have to be the biggest piece of shit in the world to get him off my back. And I can't be that guy.

But I know where to find him.

I DON'T KNOCK ON the door. I punch it three times. I hear him coming to answer it. He opens up. I want to say something, but I can't find the words. He stares back at me. He takes a drag on his cigarette, throws it to the floor, and grinds it out with his boot. It looks less like he's smiling and more like he's baring his teeth.

"Come on in, *pichón*," says my old man.

# PART 3
# CROSSES

# 20.

My old man stubs out his fifth cigarette in a wooden ashtray. The butts pointing upwards look like flowers in a garden of ash.

"We can fix this," he says.

He leans back and rests his arms on the cracked and torn leather sofa which, at first glance, looks like the most cared-for item in the house. The cement wall is pocked with damp spots, and a few nails stick out here and there. My old man picks up a coffee cup with a broken handle. He always broke them off because his fingers were too big to fit. He takes a sip and puts the mug back onto a table made of a piece of plywood and a beer crate. He stares at me. I look at his face and his wrinkles. His eyes look like bullet holes in a cracked window, and when he smiles, it breaks into even more shards.

"Let's be clear," I say. "This isn't going to end with the two of us hugging and ringing in the new year together or any of that shit."

"I thought you already knew I don't do hugs."

"You don't do checking up on us either, but you came and found me when you got out of jail. Maybe somebody in there forced a little love into you."

"You're funnier than I thought. You barely talked as a kid, you'd just sit there and look around. We thought you were mute or something."

He puts another cigarette between his lips. He rolls his Zippo back and forth across his jeans in a smooth movement to light it, then lifts it to his cigarette.

"If you'd ever come to visit me you'd have known I was about to get out." He puffs smoke out his nose. "A few weeks before they let me out this guy Martillo from the same block came and told me a few assholes were running around saying they were going to do me in. That wasn't the first time some dumb piece of shit wanted to win himself a medal by taking me out and ended up with a scar instead.

"I won't bore you with the details, but two of them got carried out in bags. The other one made it because the guards showed up. I must have given him some brain damage though, because he thought it was a great idea to go and say I'd started the whole thing. I could forget about parole. So I went and looked him up. 'My cell wall's all full of scratches to count off the days,' I told him. 'So now you're going to help me keep count. And if you think about saying something, well, let's just say if I can't count the days anymore, neither can you.' So every night I'd go in with a shiv and cut another day into his skin. Four years of that shit. Can you imagine what the little fuck looked like after that? Like a zebra. That was the closest thing I got to love on the inside."

"I don't give a fuck about your stories. All I want is for you to help me with this. I don't care about any of the shit you did or didn't do, or if you feel bad about it, and I definitely don't want you to say you're sorry."

He shakes his head and waves his hand at me. He blows out some smoke and plants another cigarette butt in the ashtray. They're the flowers that would grow around his grave if anyone ever cared enough to bury him.

"Get yourself a glass of whiskey, *pichón*," he says. "I hope you're done because I've got some calls to make. You just make yourself comfortable and let me take care of this."

When he gets up I can see, hanging from a nail, a wooden sign carved with what could be our family motto: RAISE CROSSES AND YOU WILL HAVE A CEMETERY.


**JUST LIKE IN THE** old days. Them talking out on the patio and me waiting inside.

They've been talking for half an hour. They're burning through one cigarette after the other. The butts haven't even hit the weeds that reach their knees, and my old man's already got the Zippo out and they're lighting another one. They're sitting on iron chairs at a marble table. It's like no time has passed at all. The other guy looks just like his dad.

He has short black hair and is wearing a polo shirt unbuttoned to show off a gold chain. The Rolex on his wrist is worth just a little less than the house. Now he's the one talking.

I take another sip of instant coffee. I try to see what time it is, but there's no TV, and the clock I see on the kitchen wall hasn't worked since they put my old man away. There's a bowed 1987 almanac hanging next to a burnt curtain. From the door of his room, I can see the red numbers on the alarm clock telling me that in three hours I'm supposed to be delivering a girl.

I put my hand in my pocket. Behind the modeling agency card, I find the card for the hotel where I dropped off my sister-in-law and niece yesterday. "It's just for tonight, Vivi," I told her. "Until I'm sure everything's okay." I want to call them, but there's no phone, and everything's far from okay. So I go back into the living room and sit down and wait.

My old man takes a last drag on his cigarette. The other guy's has turned into a grey worm between his fingers. He's still talking, and my old man's listening carefully. He nods, and they both stand up. Samuel puts a hand on the other man's shoulder and says something. The guy laughs, puts out his right hand, and they shake, like they've just signed an agreement.

When they come in, I can see that the guy's belt buckle is engraved with the initials DP. He doesn't even bother to look at me. I'm nothing to him. I don't even live in Misiones to be able to vote for him. My old man opens the door for him. The black Mazda is still outside. The guy in a suit leaning against the hood turns and opens the door for Senator Anibal Di Pietro, Jr.

I wait until the sound of the motor disappears, and only then do I open my mouth.

"What did he say?"

My old man grabs the mug and finishes off what's left of the coffee.

"It's all set." He runs his hands along the rips in the sofa and pulls out a little stuffing. "Anibalito's going to have to put down some *pirá piré* and pull some strings, but he'll get Seba out. As long as we do him a favor."

"What does he want?"

He drops his gaze and turns the mug on the table.

"He wants us to help him with a problem he's got with a mutual friend," he says, standing up. He takes down the wooden sign. Hanging on the same nail is a set of keys. He grabs them and goes into his room.

The words *Paraguayan gig* flash in my brain.

I hear the legs of the bedframe scraping across the wooden floor. The jingling of the keys. Then comes the creak of a tin lid opening, a metallic yawn. He comes back with a tackle box in each hand and sets them on the table. He opens them up, and it's not regular bait I see inside. From one, he takes out two Glocks and a .38 long with a wooden stock. From the other, a sawed-off shotgun. He puts in the first shell, closes his eyes, and smiles. When he opens them, he looks at me and says:

"He wants us to flood the Paraná with Centurión's blood."

# 21.

The red dirt road winds down from the bank like a tongue, ending at the door of the hotel. The neon sign washes my sister-in-law in green light. The wind moves her hair, and a few wisps blow into her eyes. She catches them in her hand and holds them against the side of her face so she can look, once again, at the Escort with tinted windows parked a few yards away with the driver leaning against the trunk.

"Everything's going to be fine," I say. "It's just to be on the safe side."

"Don't lie to me."

"Could you do me a favor and just get in the car?"

"Tell me what's going on."

I scratch my neck. There's dirt stuck to the sweat. A trucker comes out of the hotel and gets into a Scania sitting in the parking lot. He starts it up.

"What the hell is going on, Tomás?"

Violeta comes out to stand behind her mother. She's wearing a dress and new sneakers. They were a Christmas present. I went with Seba to buy them the last day we were together before all of this happened. We'd also looked at a ring for Viviana, but he didn't have enough for it. I wanted to lend him some money, but he said, "Forget about it. When I get back, I'll be able to buy her a ring so big she'll need to start lifting weights to be able to wear it."

"Uncle Tomás. What are you doing here?"

"I came over to say hi." I squat down to give her a hug.

"Did you bring me my present?"

"I forgot it," I say, but my sister-in-law opens her mouth at the same time and says I did.

Lelé smiles.

"What is it?"

"When your uncle really loves somebody, he gives them a ticket to go somewhere."

"Where are we going?" Lelé asks, excited.

"To Oberá, honey."

"Oberá?"

"I'll let you pick where next time," I say. "Now go wait over there, I've got to finish talking to your mom."

She sits down on a peeling bench.

"Why do we have to go?" My sister-in-law strafes like a machine gun. "Didn't you do what they wanted?"

"And then some," I say. "But your husband had a lot of unfinished business."

She swallows and doesn't say anything else. Her loose hair blows in the wind, and when she looks at the highway, the strands draw brown bars across her face. I'm not sure if it's because of the wind, but her eyes are shining. I put a hand on her shoulder and give her a few pats.

"I'm taking care of it, Vivi. And the longer you take to get in the car, the longer it's going to take me."

The motor of the Scania revs up, and the car moves away. My sister-in-law closes her eyes and shakes her head. She points at my old man, leaning on the hood of the Fairlane with a cigarette. The smoke coming out of his mouth looks like cotton.

"Goddamn it," she says. "If he's here, that means everything went to hell."

"If he's here, it means I'm doing absolutely everything I can to sort this out. So do me a favor and get in the fucking car."

Viviana exhales through her nose and laughs.

"One day with him, and you're already talking like that."

"I picked that up from Seba's friends."

I raise my hand to the driver of the Escort and point to Viviana's bag on the ground. He leans over to pick it up, but she stops him.

"I can get it," she says. "Come on, Lelé."

My niece comes over. Her mother takes her arm and puts her in the car. The door slams. The Escort starts up and drives off in the other direction. My old man takes a last drag and throws his cigarette on the ground. The final bit of sunset is swallowed up by the horizon.

"She's a handful," he says when I walk over. He gets into the Fairlane and reaches over to open the door for me. I sit down, and he starts the engine. "I'd be mad, too. Seba's in Candelaria. That's a rough joint. But not nearly as rough as Oberá."

We get going.

A red cloud erases everything behind us.

WE DRIVE BY THE address Gamarra gave me to drop off the girl. In the middle of a lot is a big structure with cement walls, a tin roof, and windows filled in with cinderblocks. You'd think it was just an unfinished building if it weren't for the door with more locks on it than a Houdini trick.

My old man drives by and parks the Fairlane at a truck-stop *parrilla* fifty yards farther on with the car pointing out toward the street.

Samuel goes inside the Kesman Brothers Meat Palace. Five minutes later, he comes back out with a bag and tosses it into the back seat. He turns on the radio. A *chamamé* is playing. A bulb comes on at the front of the cement building, lighting up the 2276 painted next to the door. I can see an F100 out back in the weeds with wooden sides on the bed. Everything around looks about the same. Lots with fallen fences, thrown-together constructions with DIRECTV antennas here and there. And then, where the road becomes a highway downhill, nothing.

The clock says there's an hour left til the delivery. I look at the grey clouds and see my old man again, a few hours before, explaining what's been going on.

"CENTURIÓN BURNED HIS BRIDGES over in Paraguay," he'd said as he cleaned the barrel of a disassembled 9mm, the last of the seven guns he'd gotten ready. "After the attack on the Di Pietro crew, he knew they'd come after him. He left a few nobodies in his whorehouse and moved here, where's he's still got some connections." He set aside the cotton covered in gunpowder residue and looked at me through the barrel like a spyglass. "Nobody knows where he is. Except his people."

He kept talking as he poked another bit of cotton into the barrel.

"Everything would have been a hell of a lot easier if your shit-for-brains brother knew which team to play for. One call to the Di Pietros and he would have been sitting pretty right here, but now we have to go and knock off that piece of shit. Di Pietro's people knew he worked with Centurión, but they thought as soon as he started with them, he'd stopped running with Centurión. But no. Seba had to play both sides, and the Di Pietros weren't too happy about that. They were even less happy after a couple of attacks on their camps, and not just because Seba knew about it ahead of time and didn't say anything, but because he must have been there shooting at them, too." Samuel clicked his tongue. "Loyalty was never your brother's strong suit."

He finished putting together the 9mm. On the table, the dirty cotton balls piled on top of each other looked like storm clouds, like he'd shot down the sky and it was lying dead at our feet. I thought that would be the closest my old man would ever get to heaven.

**A TRUCK BLOWS ITS** horn and disappears down the dirt road. Samuel turns down the radio and lights a cigarette.

"I wish they'd hurry up. I'm hungry," he says.

"What's that?" I say, gesturing to the bag with sandwiches at the back seat.

"An alibi."

He lifts up his shirt and shows me the round scar on his stomach.

"A shot from a .38. Compared to the hole the last sandwich I ate here burned into me, this is nothing."

A dark-haired girl in a crop top comes out with a truck driver. When she gets into a parked Scania, her skirt rides up and shows her white panties.

"Seba got better taste in *guainas*," he says. "He dated some ugly-ass girls when he was a kid. It seemed like the fewer teeth they had, the more he liked them. The other day I ran into the first girl he brought home. You remember Araceli?"

"I remember how pissed Seba was when you kicked her out of the house."

"It's a damn good thing I did. The little shit was thirteen and thought that cow was the love of his life. But I was on to her. That little bitch wanted to get herself a man and ride it out her whole life. She's thirty now and already has grandkids. So she proved me right."

"Seba isn't doing much better."

"I didn't tell him to start working with Centurión."

"When they put you away, the list Alvarenga brought over wasn't of stuff to pick up at the supermarket."

"A couple of fucking names. He could have taken them out with a slingshot. It's not my fault Seba had a taste for gore."

I turn up the radio. My old man looks at the front of the restaurant, blows out a lungful of smoke, and turns the volume down.

"Listen," he says. "This thing . . . this whole mess, I mean . . . I can take care of it on my own . . . What I'm saying is . . ." He scratches his neck. "You don't have to get your hands dirty."

He squeezes the wheel. His veins look like high-tension wires.

"I promised Seba I'd take care of it. And that's what I'm going to do."

Christmas lights come on in the window of Kesman Brothers, reflecting off the cars in the parking lot.

"And anyway," I say, "my hands are already dirty."

My old man lets go of the wheel and looks at me.

"Looks like you boys didn't turn out so bad after all."

"No thanks to you, that's for sure."

He snorts and shakes his head.

"You're just as sore as you were when you were a kid," he says. "Mad at the world. You should get yourself a *guaina*, maybe learn to smile. You should know by now a girl'll do more to save you than a bullet-proof vest."

"You can teach me how to shoot, what gun I should use, and how to gut somebody. But it's a little fucking late for fatherly advice. Especially from a guy who's longest-lasting relationship was with his gun."

"I never had trouble getting pussy. Still don't."

I take a deep breath and let it out.

"And did you treat your gun the same way you treated Mom? I'll never understand how she put up with you so long."

"That bitch doesn't deserve to be called Mom."

"You never tried to find her when she left."

"Oh, I tried, and I found her. You were pretty little when you asked me what happened to your mom, so maybe you didn't understand when I told you your mom had changed you kids up for other boys. Now that you're all grown up maybe you'll get it."

He sucks on his cigarette and blows the smoke out against the roof.

"I wanted blowjobs, not kids. In my line of work, a kid means this shit." He points at the cement house. "Something they can threaten you with. But your mom wanted kids, so I caved. I never did something stupid out of hate, but I've sure done stupid shit for other reasons. And I don't mean you two, I mean caring about that bitch. The night your mom took off, the only things she left behind were a turd in the toilet and the two of you. Think about it."

A blue Senda parks next to us, and a couple gets out with a little girl, each of them holding one of her hands. They lift her up, and her feet wave in the air before they put her back down on the gravel.

"That night when I went to do a line and realized your mom had taken all the coke was the only time I thought of her. After a little while I found out that instead of breast-feeding you, she was letting a bunch of bikers suck her tits for coke. That's when I realized how your mom loved kids: as raw sperm, when she could guzzle them down. Not when they cried or wanted something to eat. You can hate me, and you'd be right. I'm all the shit you can think to call me. But I stayed, kiddo."

"You should have left, too."

My jaw pops. Pain radiates from the base of my ear to wrap around my head like a turban. My old man rolls down the window, flicks out his cigarette butt, then rolls it back up.

"So I might be a son of a bitch. But you're a son of a whore."

I punch the glove box. The only thing moving at the cement house are the weeds swaying in the wind. The gusts bend them so far that the tips touch the ground. Samuel lights another cigarette.

"I always thought you'd have a few kids," he says. "When you were little you had this way of looking at girls that they couldn't keep from smiling."

"Could you shut the fuck up? I think you're the one who doesn't get it. So here it is: if you were on fire, I'd throw gas on you."

"Then I might want to give you a hug. Who knows, maybe you'll get your chance now."

He gets out.

"What are you doing?" I ask.

He opens up the trunk, and I can't see him. I stick the Colt into my pants, cover it with my shirt and get out of the car. Samuel takes a gas can and walks toward the cement house. I can see the two 9mm pistols at his back sticking out under his shirt like bones.

"What are you doing?" I say again and follow him, looking left and right to see if anyone's watching us. The only person outside is the dark-haired girl getting out of the truck and touching up her lipstick.

My old man goes onto the lot. The weeds swallow up his legs, then mine. I catch up to him. A cigarette hangs from his lips, and the ash drops away. A car comes toward the house, slowly. We lose sight of it behind the side wall.

It reappears and speeds up. Samuel hugs the back corner of the house and waves to me to stop. From inside, we can hear cumbia music. My old man shakes his head and pulls out one of the nines. He leans out to take a look, then waves for me to follow him. Out back of the house, the weeds disappear, leaving a bald spot on the ground. Next to the F100 is a rope with clothes hanging from it. Sheets and some shirts and torn boxers, and a Cerro Porteño jersey. Next to a door with as many bars as the one out front is a pile of beer crates and bags with the Kesman Brothers logo.

"Check in the back," he says, motioning with his chin at the F100.

I lift the latch and open the back of the truck. It looks like the back seat of a cop car, but it's closer to a livestock truck. There are handcuffs screwed into the wood with chains that hang like rosaries from the walls, strips of cloth for gags, and a few ropes.

"Nothing," I tell him.

"Move over," he says, starting to coat the F100 with gas, all without tossing away his cigarette. "Go off to the side there. When they come out, let them have it."

I want to tell him okay, but all I can do is nod. I get in position. The sound of cumbia is still coming from inside the house. The smell of grass disappears in the gas fumes. He takes another drag on the cigarette and looks at the F100. We walk closer. A gust of wind billows the clothes on the line. He opens the door of the truck, gets inside, and grabs a black cap. He puts it on and asks me how he looks. I shrug. He looks in the rearview mirror of the truck and gives me a thumbs up.

"Give me a rag."

I go around the back of the truck to get one of the rags. When I walk by the clothesline, I have another idea. I pull down the Cerro Porteño jersey and pass it to him.

"I hope it's his favorite," my old man says.

"It is."

He soaks the jersey in gas. He shakes the can and shows me what's left inside.

"Here's your chance," he says, offering it to me.

I click my tongue and he laughs. He throws the rest on the jersey and lights it using his Zippo. He throws it, and it lands on top of the hood. The flames jump up in a wall of fire that starts to grow and engulf the F100. The tarp covering the back takes a moment to catch, but it finally does and holes start to appear in it. The whole cab is on fire, and the wood slats on the back make the truck look like a match until the flames reach the gas tank and it explodes. My face is covered in sweat. Through the flames, I can see my old man with a gun in his hand.

The iron door opens and bounces off the cement wall.

"Fuck," says the first one who comes out. I don't have time to see if I know him. My old man's shot goes in one side of his face and comes out the other. He falls forward, against the F100. The flames spread across his clothes, and he starts to burn.

The guy coming out after him manages to jump to one side and avoid one of my old man's bullets and one of mine. He ducks back inside. Samuel runs after him. He makes it to the door in two steps and shoots inside.

"Come on, come on," he says, running in.

The door leads into a hallway. In the middle is the guy who managed to get back inside, two bullet holes in his back, and one in his head. There's a door on the right. I try to open it, but it's locked. A guy in boxers leans out from around a corner and shoots at us, along with two of his buddies. We flatten ourselves against the wall. The cement bursts above my old man's head and falls into his hair, turning it even greyer. Samuel pulls the trigger until he hears a click. In the same movement, he drops the empty pistol and with his left hand, he pulls out the other 9mm and keeps firing. I hear a muffled scream, a door slamming, then cumbia. We go into what would have been a living room. The guy is sitting with his legs spread and his back to the wall. His exploded head is red graffiti on the cement. My old man points to a door on the right and heads over to it. I walk toward the hall and see them go out the door that was locked. One of them doesn't even bother to look back. A shot from the Colt tears the flesh from the bone in his shoulder, and he falls face first to the ground outside. The other one stops short to keep from running into the burning F100. He hesitates. I shoot for his legs. I miss. Once. Twice. The guy turns around: it's Cerro Porteño, shirtless but with the club's crest tattooed on his chest. One shot from my old man ruins his foot, and he falls to the side as if someone had pulled a rug out from under him.

The two guys are right next to each other. The flames make our shadows dance. Cerro Porteño grabs his foot and writhes around. The one I got in the shoulder rolls over. Froth is coming out of his mouth like he's a beer can.

"Which one is any good to us?" my old man asks.

I push my foot down on Cerro Porteño's balls, and he curls up.

"This one."

My old man nods and feeds the other one a bullet. A stream of blood comes out of his mouth, washing away the froth.

"Go get the car," says my old man.

I avoid the people who came out to see what was going on and start up the Fairlane. When I get back, my old man is pushing Cerro Porteño's foot up against the scalding door of the F100. There's a smell of burnt meat.

"I don't want him bleeding all over my trunk," he says.

# 22.

The headlights of the Fairlane light up Samuel opening a gate lost in a field of weeds. The thumps in the trunk shake the car, and when I turn on the radio, they mix in with the drums of a folklore song and disappear.

"I liked the other music better," says my old man when he gets back in.

He turns off the radio, and we can hear the sounds from the trunk again. Trees start to appear along the side of the road until we come to a wooden house painted white with a border of red dust around the bottom. Out front, two dogs emerge from behind a shed and run to greet us. My old man shoos them away. The screen door of the house opens and out comes Alvarenga, shirtless, wearing running shorts and his fanny pack. He and my old man look at each other and smile.

"It's been a while, *chera'a*," says Samuel, and they hug.

"It's been a while, brother," says Alvarenga when they let go. The thumps and shouts interrupt the reunion.

"We brought a visitor. Do you still have the pigs?"

"Out back."

"I hope they like Paraguayan meat," he says, opening the trunk. Cerro Porteño's hands and feet are tied with rope, and there's a black bag over his head. Samuel pulls him out and drops him on the ground.

"Fucking *kurepí*," the Paraguayan yells. My old man buries his boot in his chest.

"Now that word I know. I might be a pig-skinned son of a bitch, but you're about to meet some real pigs."

"This asshole again?" says Alvarenga when Samuel cuts the bag with his knife and Cerro Porteño's face appears.

"*Nde añarokópeguare!*"

"I can't understand a goddamn word you're saying, kid, but once you and I are through, we'll understand each other just fine. You still got everything set up?"

"Like always, brother. My slaughterhouse is your slaughterhouse."

Samuel starts to drag Cerro Porteño toward the shed.

"Let me do it," I say. Alvarenga and my old man swivel their heads around to look at me. Cerro Porteño keeps writhing around.

"You sure, *pichón*?"

I nod.

"You think we should give them to him?" he asks Alvarenga.

"The gloves are right where you hung them up the last time."

"What gloves?"

"A little help," says my old man, letting go of Cerro Porteño. I grab his rope and haul him over to the shed.


I HIT HIM ONCE, then again. The Paraguayan, hanging from a chain like a side of beef, shakes with each impact. I tighten up my old man's "little help" on my hands: a pair of gloves with pieces of sandpaper and ground-up glass glued to the knuckles. Cerro Porteño's face is scraped off and melting onto the floor. There are pieces of broken teeth at his feet and cigarette butts next to my old man's boots.

"Just let me know when you're tired."

I wipe away the sweat with my arm. My knuckles are throbbing.

"Centurión," I say to the Paraguayan again.

The answer's always the same: he laughs.

I aim for the Cerro Porteño crest on his chest and give him a one-two then a hook to the face. He only opens his mouth to spit out another piece of tooth.

My old man taps his right foot faster and faster.

"This is how long my patience lasts," he says, holding up his half-smoked cigarette to Cerro Porteño.

I hit him with everything I've got. His chest caves in, a rib breaks. The abrasions eat across his skin like fungus, turning him into a dalmation with red spots. A loyal dog.

My old man's cigarette goes flying and is snuffed out in

the puddle of Cerro Porteño's blood. He takes off his cap, then his shirt, and hangs them on a meathook. He cracks his knuckles.

"Go get something to drink," he says to me.

I take off the gloves and hold them out to him. He waves them away and opens up a tackle box. He starts taking things out and arranging them on top of a tree trunk. A toothbrush. A long knife, and a short one with a cross engraved into the bone handle. Cerro Porteño isn't laughing anymore.

"Decisions aren't your thing, man," he says. "I've lost count of how many guys we've brought here. Some of them sang right away, like a goddamn opera. We had to work pretty hard on others, I won't lie to you. There were some tough nuts to crack, but there's a reason why the ground around here is the reddest anywhere in this province."

My old man sharpens a knife against a stone.

"Off you go," he says. "Alvarenga makes a great fucking Negroni. Actually, go tell him to make one for each of us. And on your way out, plug this in for me," he says, handing me the end of an extension cord. "The saying goes that to get to the truth, you've got to get to the heart of a man," he continues. "There are a few ways to do that, but my favorite's a knife. Or a drill bit. Bad decisions, man. Bad decisions. You should have gotten yourself some body armor instead of that stupid fucking crest tattoo," he says, landing two punches on his chest. My old man puts Cerro Porteño's gag back in his mouth. "Now I'm going to choose when you sing. Let's dance, *chamigo*. Let's dance."

With Cerro Porteño's first muffled cry, I walk out the door of the shed dragging the extension cord behind me. One of the dogs licks at the blood on my hands. Alvarenga's next to the door with the table all laid out: bottles of gin, Martini Rosso, and Campari, and a plate with a couple of lines of coke.

"How's it going?" he asks, as if I'd just come from a soccer game.

I show him the extension cord, and he smiles.

"Over there." He points and then leans over the plate. I plug it in. "I hope he doesn't blow the fuse, the fight starts soon."

He rubs his face a little and sniffs.

"They double-crossed me in Paraguay, *gurí*. They told me they'd already sent you back here, that everything was all set. Those fucks." He pauses to squeeze his nostrils and sniff again. "Your old man got me up to speed. What a fucking mess. But don't worry, we'll sort it out."

"Is Di Pietro all out of lackeys? We've got to be his troops now?"

"We took them all out. The ones we plugged on Christmas were the last of them. Centurión and his little crack team went from bunker to bunker."

"Does he know it was us?"

"Do you think your old man's that stupid? They think

your brother took a few out, but that doesn't matter anymore. As long as we take care of this."

I look at my split knuckles. Another muffled cry comes from the shed. It sounds like an animal about to be sacrificed. Alvarenga snorts another line, then a third.

"Did he ask for his Negroni yet?" he asks me with a stiff smile.

He opens a styrofoam cooler and puts two ice cubes unto a whiskey glass, and a few more into a bigger one.

"The key to a good drink is the same as the key to a good torture session: don't go too far." He takes out a metal cocktail jigger and fills it with gin. "Gin's the cornerstone, *gurí*, it's like wearing black or cutting off somebody's fingers. It's a sure thing." He pours the gin into the larger glass and measures out a jigger of Martini Rosso. "But watch out. If you pour too much, it's too strong, and if you go overboard with the knife, you end up with nothing. Balance, kid." He pours the Campari and stirs the drink up with a knife. The red in the glass grows more intense.

"Did he ever go too far?" I ask.

He puts his hand over the top of the whiskey glass and turns it over to let the melted water drip out. Then he pours the drink into the smaller glass.

"If God had blood, this'd be it. Take that in to him, *gurí*."

"Is that it? Don't you want me to take him some of that, too?" I say, pointing at the bag of coke.

"That's your old man's favorite drug," Alvarenga says, nodding at the shed. "Hurry up, if the ice melts it ruins it."

When I go in, Cerro Porteño tries to look at me, but the blood running from the cuts in his eyebrows blinds him. The rag in his mouth shakes like a clumsy tongue. There's a dotted red line around the crest tattoo. *Cut here.* It looks like one of those images of a saint's bleeding heart. Samuel sticks the knife into the tree trunk and walks over to me. He takes the drink from my hand and empties it in two swallows.

"Damn. I missed those." He hands the glass back to me. His fingerprints are stamped on the glass in red. "Did you plug that in?"

I say yes and turn around.

"I'm going to start counting. Whenever you want, you stop me," he says to Cerro Porteño. "One, two three." The Paraguayan shakes his head. "Okay, three. Decisions really aren't your thing, man."

Before I make it outside, I hear a drill. As I set the glass on the table, a scream drowns out the sound of the drill bit.

"This is for you," Alvarenga says and hands me a Negroni.

"He's going to overdo it," I say, sitting down.

"Are you going to tell Monzón how to punch?"

The screams get louder, like a singer warming up.

"I wonder which one he chose," says Alvarenga

"Three."

He winces and shuts his eyes

"What the hell is it?"

"You don't want to know, kid."

He sticks his snout into his own Negroni and finishes it off. The screaming starts to fade into the background and mix with the sound of the crickets. I sip my drink and let the alcohol help calm me down. I wipe my face with a handkerchief, and my brow's sweaty again in minutes. It's so hot I can barely breathe.

"You don't know how happy it makes me to have the three of us here together. I always dreamed of the four of us, all sitting down to eat together."

"You're going to have to keep on dreaming."

"You don't think we can get Seba out?"

"Oh, I think we can do that."

He shakes his head, sniffs, and starts to mix another Negroni.

"So I bet in your mind your old man's the bad guy, right?" he says. "With that attitude, you're not going to hang on to that girl from Buenos Aires. If she put up with what happened the other day, she's a keeper."

Women, keeping them. I take out my wallet and touch Anyelén's chain. I look at her name engraved on it and put the chain back, next to Gamarra's bullet. As I do, my brother's face becomes even more deformed, crushed against the plastic protector like he wants to escape.

"I need you to find something out for me," I say.

"I live to serve."

The Paraguayan's screams force me to lean in close to

Alvarenga so he can hear me. When I finish talking, the door to the shed opens and my old man walks out wiping an even spray coating of blood off his chest with a towel. In his other hand is a shred of flesh with the Cerro Porteño crest tattoo.

"This is too bitter for the pigs," he says.

He takes the Negroni from Alvarenga's hand and throws it back.

"What did he say?" I ask.

"He called me all the same pet names you do. And he also told me everything he knew." He rubs the towel across the back of his neck, then scrubs his face. "Commissioner Odriozola. That's the guy who was in with Centurión to put Seba away. And he knows where to go to pick up the bribes that keep the Centurión crew's businesses open."

I put my head in my hands.

"Goddamn it."

"Don't worry about it. Odriozola is an old friend."

Alvarenga laughs.

"You think he still remembers me?"

"I sure wouldn't forget somebody who took one of my old man's eyes out," says Alvarenga.

I punch the table. The bottle of gin wobbles, and Samuel catches it before it falls.

"Don't worry," my old man says. "Tomorrow I'll make the two of them match. We're not going to feed any cop meat to the pigs. Wouldn't want to turn them into cannibals." He sits down. "Make another Negroni, *chera'a*, this calls for a toast."

Alvarenga hands us each a drink. He and Samuel raise their glasses. I take mine, throw the whole thing back, and put the glass back on the table upside-down, the two ices cubes dancing over the table like eyeballs. I worry if I will be able to look back and remember things the way they actually are. If I ever have been, at any point in my life.

"Night," I say and go inside.

# 23.

What wakes you up at Alvarenga's place out in the country isn't a rooster crowing. It's the sound of the pigs crunching away on some guy who made bad decisions. This time it was Cerro Porteño. Through a slit in the shutter, I can see a snout smeared in red dust eating something so chewed up it's impossible to tell if it was an arm or a leg.

When Seba and I were kids, we used to spend the night here all the time. More than once my old man locked himself inside the shed, and when I asked Alvarenga what he was doing, he told me he was getting the food ready for the pigs. Back then I had a pretty different idea of what Samuel did.

The bed where my brother used to sleep is empty. It's made up with threadbare sheets and a blanket of dust. I can see him looking at me, waiting for me to wake up. "Get up, Tommy." Then we'd skip breakfast and go outside to play soccer. I imagine him in jail, waiting for my visit. "It won't be long now, Seba," I say to the emptiness and get up.

There are bottles like melted candles sitting between them. *Truco* scores are scrawled on butcher paper. An army of flies buzzes around a black rind of cheese and the skin of a salami.

"Pass," says my old man.

Alvarenga makes down a point, and they're tied at three *buenas*. He shuffles. The cards are worn, and when I see a mark on one, I realize it's the same deck they've been playing with for as long as I can remember.

"Morning."

Alvarenga passes him the deck to cut.

"Just made," he says, pouring me a cup of coffee from an old percolator.

I take two sips. It's strong. I wipe the sleep out of my eyes. Samuel's wearing an unbuttoned plaid shirt and a worn pair of jeans he didn't have on yesterday. Alvarenga puts the deck back together and deals. Neither of them looks like they slept, but they don't seem tired or high. I finish the coffee and leave the cup on the table.

"I don't want to interrupt the tournament, but we've got to go find this guy."

"Have another cup of coffee, *gurí*," Alvarenga says.

My old man gathers up his cards and arranges them in a fan in his right hand.

"Let's see here. *Envido*," he says.

"Did you say *envido*?"

Samuel laughs.

"*Real envido*, then."

"You've got that much?"

"Sometimes you get what you want," my old man says.

"You're full of shit." Alvarenga looks at his cards again. "*Falta envido.*"

"You got nothing, *chera'a.*"

"Neither do you."

"What do you think?" He tries to show me the cards in his hand, but I don't look and he ends up saying, "I'll take it."

"Son of a bitch," Alvarenga says. "Show them."

Samuel puts down the seven of cups. Alvarenga throws his cards on the table face-down and the flies jump into the air. I take another sip of coffee and fix myself a salami and cheese sandwich. In the background, I can still hear the pigs eating.

"Want to play for another point?" asks Alvarenga.

My old man gathers up the cards and sets them off to one side. He looks at me.

"When we get back," he says.

"How are we going to find this guy?" I ask.

"Well, probably not by sitting here jerking off." He pours himself a cup of coffee. "Tell me, who would you trust? A friend, or some guy you've got by the balls?"

"A friend."

"Neither of them," he says. "But if you have to trust somebody, trust the people who are scared of you. Think about it. How many times have you been let down by people you love, and how many times by people who are terrified of you? I'd rather be feared than loved. Being loved is over-rated."

"Where are you going with all this?"

"I've got two pieces of information. One's about a guy I know . . . and the other is about someone who's not going to want to let me down: Sergeant Iturrioz." He takes another sip of coffee. "This blonde I see sometimes gave me pictures of a cop having a little party with a girl who went straight from sucking on her mom's tit to sucking cock. It turns out Iturrioz knows where to find his boss. They used to be buddies and go to the same parties. I say we go that route," he says, going inside the house.

I look at Alvarenga and ask him what Samuel's talking about. He takes a military shirt off the back of his chair and puts it on. He waves his hand to tell me not to worry about it, then comes over to me and says:

"I checked on what you asked about. They'll let me know as soon as anything turns up."

My old man comes back wearing his cap, his plaid shirt buttoned up, and a worn jacket. He puts two shotguns in the trunk like fishing rods.

"We're going fishing, boys."

WE DRIVE NEXT TO the Paraná on Route 12. My old man's behind the wheel. Alvarenga rides in back and whistles something that sounds like a tango and looks out the window. The trees move in the wind beyond the dirt shoulder. Red waves rise and eddy. The sun burns the edges of grey clouds. The rays bounce off the hood of the Fairlane, which keeps accumulating miles. We pass a truck hump-backed with sacks of *yerba mate*. The smell fills the car. The heavy, wet heat is like another passenger.

A road snakes off to the left and disappears in the pines. My old man looks at Alvarenga, who nods at him. He slows down, then cuts into the weeds about a hundred yards farther on. He finds a clearing in the trees and shuts off the engine. The sound of the birds reminds me of the shrieks in the jungle. Me and Anyelén running.

"So?" says my old man, already outside the car. "You want to stay here?"

I peel myself off the seat and follow them. The ground is wet, and butterflies flit around between the tree trunks. An orange one flies in front of me, and when the sun hits it, its wings light up as if it's on fire. The ground starts to slope down. The current is fast, and the reflection of the pines is just a stain on the water. Fifty yards away, two men sit in folding chairs with their backs to us. My old man nods, and we keep walking. When we're ten yards away, we come straight at them from behind.

One has grey hair and a painter's brush mustache and is wearing sunglasses, a polo shirt, and plaid swim trunks. Above his Ray-Bans, his right eyebrow is split in two. The other stands and starts to reel something in. He's got on an unbuttoned grey-blue shirt, flip-flops, and black shorts, and a plastic rosary around his neck. There are another two fishing rods set into structures like tripods and a paint bucket off to one side. The three lines shimmer like the devil's saliva. The hook comes out of the water empty.

"Looks like you're having a bad day, Odriozola," says my old man.

The two of them jump and look around. The rod falls from the second man's hands like a broken branch, and he raises his arm to block the sun from his eyes.

"Who's that?" asks the oldest one.

"I understand if you don't recognize me, sir. I know you've had some problems with your eyesight. But your son not knowing who I am, well, that just breaks my heart."

Commissioner Odriozola puts down his hands. His Adam's apple throbs. The wind billows his shirt and rosary, and the butt of his police-issue is visible at his waist. The one-eyed old man touches a couple of tackle boxes on a folding stool.

"Don't move," says Samuel. "I'd hate for you to have another accident."

Alvarenga stands between the two of them. Odriozola looks at the pines behind us.

"So little Tincho made commissioner. To think he'd just gotten his badge when you and I were at it. You set him up right. It's true that the shell doesn't fall far from the gun."

"Just stay calm," says Odriozola.

"Do I look nervous to you?"

My old man looks at the floats fifty yards downriver next to the dry branches of a tree buried in the water.

"Some quality father-son time, huh? Nothing better than fishing. You know what they say: a fishing line . . ."

"Is a life line," Alvarenga finishes.

"Although I heard it's against the law to fish here without a permit. I'd like to think the two of you, being officers of the law, have one, right?"

One-eye's stomach looks like a toad about to burst. The white hair curls on his chest. Above his Ray-Bans, his right eyebrow is split in two. When Alvarenga opens his fanny pack, the old man flinches. Alvarenga shows him a cigarette and a Zippo.

"I'm having some quality family time, too," Samuel says. "Well, with as much of my family as I could bring."

I walk closer and look into the paint bucket. There are two dead fish inside, big ones. My old man comes over and looks at them, too.

"You've got to throw them back, friend," he says. Odriozola doesn't move. He keeps staring at the pine trees behind us. Samuel snaps his fingers, and only then does he look at him. "What is it? You're still short even with all the *pirá piré* you get from Centurión and you have to fish to eat?"

"I didn't know," says Odriozola.

My old man holds up his hand for Odriozola to shut up.

Alvarenga takes a drag on his cigarette, and the smoke filters away into the grey clouds.

"Don't worry, you're about to have the time to tell me everything. What are you fishing for? Mangus, dorados?" The father and son look at each other. "What, you're not just blind, you're mute, too?"

"Dorados," says One-eye.

"There are better places to fish from the coast than this. You should really check out Caraguata Island. There's a whirlpool down there, it's called Vairusu. You'll get yourself a dorado every time. But the best dorado fishermen go out in boats. It's just that you boys don't like to get dirty."

The clouds pass in front of the sun, and its glint disappears from the middle of the water like a light being turned off. The line on the fishing rod farthest from us starts to jiggle.

"Can I get it?" says my old man, grabbing the rod. He pulls it back and starts to reel in the line. The tip bends. "Seems like a big one."

He keeps reeling. The Odriozolas watch me and Alvarenga. I rest my hand on the Colt and tap my thumb on the butt. Thirty yards away, a dorado jumps out of the water. Alvarenga gives a yell.

"Tire him out, tire him out," he says.

"This bastard's a fighter."

My old man keeps reeling in the line. He raises the rod, then drops it. He leans back. The fish starts to jump, once, twice, like a skipping stone. Samuel reels in a little more line until he gets the fish in close. With one hand he takes the line and lifts it up, and with the other he grabs the dorado by the gills. Without asking permission, Alvarenga reaches into the tackle box and hands my old man a pair of pliers to pull out the hook. The fish opens and closes its mouth.

"Beautiful," says Samuel as the dorado tries to wriggle away. He holds it against his chest with both hands and shows it to the Odriozolas, who barely move. My old man turns and squats down at the edge of the water. He gives the fish a kiss on the belly and lets it go.

"You've got to honor a good fight," he says, drying his hands on his shirt.

Commissioner Odriozola looks at the two fishing rods on the ground, then the one still on its stand, and takes a step forward.

"I didn't know he was your son," he says. "Centurión said he was going to send me a guy. That was it."

"Cops are the worst. You take away their badge, and it's like you cut their balls off." He turns and moves behind the one-eyed man. "I'll take care of my son," he says, looking at the commissioner. "I'm here for Centurión. I'm listening."

Odriozola swallows and looks around. His fingers open and close next to his standard-issue pistol, slowly, like the legs of a crab. My old man reaches over and grabs a three-hooked lure from the tackle box and holds it up for them to see.

"From what Iturrioz told me, your tastes haven't changed. You still like little girls who are closer to wearing diapers than thongs. And from what my *gurí* tells me, Centurión's got a few of those."

Odriozola closes his eyes and shakes his head.

"He doesn't have the cathouses anymore. He's in weed now," he says. The last fishing rod in a stand starts to wobble, but no one cares. "He's got a sawmill where he hides all the weed and coke and sends it to Buenos Aires."

"Call him up and tell him you want to meet to talk about raising prices."

"You know better than anyone these are the type of guys who call you, you don't call them. I go and pick up an envelope, that's it. I don't even see him."

"Where?" I ask.

"On Route Twenty-Three. At the San Gotardo Outlook."

"That's a big place," says Alvarenga.

"The sawmill's called Kyapi."

Odriozola lifts his head, opens his eyes wide, and shouts at the pines:

"Run!"

I catch a glimpse of someone before they disappear between the tree trunks.

"He's yours, *pichón*. All yours."

I start to run after him, following the flashes of skin I can see between the branches. I dodge the trees, and my feet sink into the soft bed of needles. I'm getting closer. I can see he's wearing blue swim trunks. I make out a 4x4 parked in the distance. The guy runs toward it, and I put on speed. I get closer. Fifteen yards. Ten. He turns and looks at me. I lose him behind a tree trunk. His face breaks up, and I think I see Anyelén. Another tree trunk appears in my way, and I lose sight of her. The image of the guy returns. He trips, and before he can get back up, I jump on top of him. I put the Colt to his back.

"Turn the fuck over."

He obeys. The red dirt stuck to his face looks like a beard. He's too young to have a real one. He's not a little kid, and not an adult yet, but he's older than Anyelén ever got to be. And his old man had something to do with that, I tell myself.

"Walk," I say and start to take him back to where his father and grandfather are.

When we reach the river, my old man says:

"Now that we've got your whole family together, we can get on with getting mine back together."

"Don't hurt him," the commissioner says to me.

"Centurión," I say, pushing the Colt against the kid's neck.

"I already told you. Kyapi. That's where I pick up the money. That's all I know."

Samuel pulls off the one-eyed man's sunglasses, and behind the right lens, a patch of burnt skin appears. The kid starts praying.

"These Ray-Bans are all scratched up," he says and throws them into the water.

"You need me," Odriozola says.

"Doesn't seem that way to me."

"Centurión didn't just ask me to put Sebastián away." He scratches his face, bites his lips. "In jail, he's going to make sure he gets a visit . . ."

"I'm listening."

"They're going to beat the shit out of him and . . . you know . . . Beat him up a different way, too." The commissioner looks down for a few seconds. The bones of my old man's jaw stand out. "But if you let us go, I can make sure that doesn't happen."

My old man snorts.

"You're making some sweet deals," he says. He looks at Alvarenga, who throws his cigarette to the ground. A drop of the kid's sweat rolls around the tip of the Colt. The youngest Odriozola's going straight from a Lord's Prayer into an Ave Maria. "You should be praying like your kid here that doesn't happen, because if they touch a hair on my son's head, I'll make sure the same thing happens to your wife. It doesn't matter how fat she's gotten because I've got guys who'd fuck a snake if they could get someone to hold it down for them, and they'd be thrilled to death to fuck that old bitch."

"I'll take care of it, I swear to god, *chamigo*. I can't get him out, but I'll make sure he's safe."

"I don't hear you praying, '*chamigo*.'"

The three of them start in together on a Lord's Prayer. The

ashen clouds come together and blot out the sun. Samuel tells them to pray louder, and "thy kingdom come" is almost a shout. My old man moves his arms like he's conducting an orchestra. The "deliver us from evil" breaks like a wave on the shore, and the "amen" seems like it will never come. Commissioner Odriozola is the only one who manages it. They all cross themselves.

"Lovely trio," says Samuel. "But I'm the only one whose will's going to be done today."

My old man takes out his 9mm and fires. The bullet goes through Odriozola's eye and bursts apart his skull. Alvarenga puts two rounds into One-eye's neck, and his body falls face-forward on the ground next to the folding chair, which falls across his body like a tent. My finger trembles on the trigger. The kid takes a step toward his father instinctively, but he already knows it's too late. I know it, too. His blood spatters my face. When his body falls, I see my old man lowering his arm. A puff of gunpowder disappears from the barrel of his nine like a dying breath. He nods to me and puts his gun back in its holster. I can't make myself nod back.

Alvarenga and Samuel throw the bodies of the grandfather and the commissioner into the river along with their things.

I'm getting closer, Seba.

I'm getting closer.

The sky reflects in the puddle of blood under the boy's face, like a cloud red breath coming out of his mouth.

"They saw our faces," Samuel would've said if I'd asked him. And it would make sense in his world. It would even make sense in mine, except there's the question of how we can carry on, seeing our own faces. I stand in front of the river, not even banking on seeing myself in the reflection of the Paraná. I spit what little saliva I have left and the image muddies. I leave before it starts to form again.

"Grab his legs," my old man says to me. He's already grabbed the kid by the armpits.

Maybe the only solution is to stop trying to see everything for what it really is, to blind all the mirrors, to wear a mask, to see nothing, hear nothing, say nothing, become nothing.

Reduce everything to a us-or-them choice.

But who is really us?

Me and my father?

No way.

There is no *us* left.

I doubt if there is even any *I* left.

I grab the kid, who barely weighs anything, no heavier than a doggie bag.

The body makes a hollow sound and bubbles as the water swallows it up.

"Let's go," says Alvarenga.

I look at the Paraná one last time. The plastic rosary bobs on the surface like a little clump of fishing floats.

# 24.

The lightning traces white roots onto a tar sky and broadens for a moment the world that ends at the edge of the Fairlane's highbeams. Everything is lashed by the rain.

Samuel squints against the headlights of an oncoming truck, the first sign of life we've seen in miles.

"Do you think what Odriozola said is true?" I ask. "About Seba getting a visit."

"If we get our asses in gear, it doesn't matter if it's true or not."

The windshield wipers can't keep up, and the drops come together to form watery snakes on the glass.

"And can we trust Di Pietro?"

"You can trust that if he's not as good as his word, he's in line right after Centurión."

Alvarenga doesn't whistle or look out the windows. His eyes are locked on the windshield, his mind somewhere far away. He opens the cylinder of his .38 and takes two bullets from his military jacket to reload it.

A bolt of lightning out in the fields illuminates a green sign that reads SAN GOTARDO OUTLOOK. To the right, walls of pine trees twenty feet high. Five minutes later, the Fairlane's headlights hit a sign carved into a tree trunk: Kyapi Sawmill. As they turn off, the last drops of light are absorbed by a dirt path that leads to a pair of warehouses. My old man brakes and clocks each side. The rain sweeps across everything. He rolls down the window and sticks out his head. The Fairlane turns, and the car's hood moves in between two rows of pines. He turns on the car's dome light as his only guide. When we can see one of the sheds again through the trees, Samuel stops and turns off the light. The wall in front of us is covered by wooden beams and stacks of fruit crates. On our other side, I can see the trunk of a Renault 12, but I can't make out what color it is.

"Any idea whose pile of shit that is?" Samuel asks.

"Definitely not Centurión's," I say. "I can't see Gamarra's white Isuzu, either."

Alvarenga opens the door and before getting out, he says: "If you want to know whether it's a shoe or a seabass, you've got to pull it out of the water."

My old man and I follow him. Samuel takes a shotgun from the trunk and holds it out to me.

"I'm fine with this," I say, showing him the Colt.

He throws it to Alvarenga, who catches it and sticks the

.38 into his waistband. My old man grabs an Ithaca. He closes the trunk, and the light disappears. Everything goes dark as we enter the Pombero's mouth.

The sound of the rain is deadened by the canopy of the trees, but when we step out from under them and settle down behind a pile of trunks, our clothes adhere to our skin like stickers. In the front wall of the shed, a gust of wind flaps a door that's been left open. A little light hangs from a cable, and against the inside wall we can see a shadow crawl. Stepping through mud and puddles, we reach the Renault 12.

"Slash them," says my old man, nodding at the car and touching his belt.

I take out my knife and stab it into two of the tires. They hiss as the air escapes. We lean against the left wall of the shed under a roof made of garbage bags. We can't hear a damn thing over the rain. My hair is stuck to my forehead and falls into my eyes. Alvarenga holds up his hand, and we stop next to the door. Lightning flashes on the field in front of us.

"I called it," we hear a high-pitched voice say.

"No way."

"You went first last time."

"You can't compare this to last time."

The thunder comes, and their voices disappear. I think one of them is Flamengo.

"The last one had more miles on her than my dad's Scania, and this one's mint."

Samuel crosses quickly and leans on the wall on the other side of the door. He looks at us and holds up his index and middle fingers, then turns his hand and leaves just the index finger raised. I have no idea what the hell it means, but Alvarenga nods. My old man nods back at him, and he goes in gun raised. We're his shadows and we split up, one to each side, as soon as we've got a toe inside the door.

"If you little bitches are too busy fighting, you're going to get fucked," Samuel says.

"Goddamnit," says Flamengo, shirtless and wearing shorts that reach past his knees. His brown belt is undone. The guy standing next to him is the one with the fuzzy eyebrows that crossed the river. He's wearing a muscle shirt, work pants, and no shoes. He takes a step to the side, looking over at a table with half a brick of compressed weed and a piece on it.

"No way, *chamigo*," says my old man.

Alvarenga grabs the pistol and sticks it in the back of his waistband, next to the .38. "You come over here too, honey," he says.

A girl at the other end of the shed, sitting on a ripped mattress on the floor, stands up and pulls down the five inches of skirt that have ridden up her thighs. She walks toward us between piles of beams and two big circular saws set five feet from each other. On our end of the warehouse, the pathway is lined with mountains of tree trunks. She keeps walking until she reaches the two guys. Ten beatings ago, she might have been pretty. She's got so many scars it looks like someone put her makeup on with a knife. Flamengo looks at her tits and closes his eyes. He swears in Guarani. My Colt is aimed at his chest.

"Hands up," Samuel says. When Flamengo obeys, his shorts make a move to fall around his ankles. "Do up your belt, I've got enough ugly to look at with this *guaina* here. If she's mint, I don't even want to think what the other one looked like."

On the girl's stomach, under her shirt, there's a scar so big that if it was from a C-section they must have taken out a baby whale. Alvarenga checks the place to make sure we're alone. Next to the mattress is a metal door that leads out back. Aside from the tree trunks and beams, there are bags of weed that look just like the ones we stole from Di Pietro. The rest of the place is one solid layer of sawdust.

"You went and told your daddy, you little *gueytesco*," says Flamengo, doing up his belt.

My old man looks at me and gives me a nod to go ahead. As I step forward, the Paraguayan moves away. I smash the butt of my Colt between his forehead.

"You know why we're here."

"You're a little late, asshole, we've already got the bitch we needed."

The Colt slams against his nose and he falls to the floor. He covers his mouth with his hands and spits out blood.

"You're acting like you're tough shit against two guys who don't even have our shoes on," says Eyebrows.

I put the Colt into my waistband and jump on him. He doesn't get his arms down before my fist in his gut doubles him over. My knee meeting his face lands him on his back. He gasps, coughs, and starts to laugh.

"At least," he says from the floor, "the girls I take across make it in one piece."

My old man grabs the back of my shirt to stop me. The two guys get to their feet. Flamengo's lip is swollen. Eyebrows is still having trouble breathing.

"As you can see, my *gurí* doesn't need his father." He takes a pack of cigarettes out of his shirt pocket. It's soaked through. He pulls out a cigarette that's broken in half, clicks his tongue, and throws it on the ground. "I've lost my patience. So we're going to do this. Come here, *guaina*."

The girl comes over, and my old man puts his hand on her back and hugs her against him.

"Do you know how to count down from ten?" he asks her. She nods. My old man makes a surprised face. "When the little Indian makes it to zero, the one who tells me where the fuck Centurión is, is going to come out of this thing better."

Flamengo shakes his head and looks at my old man's Ithaca.

"Go ahead, sweetie."

By eight, both the guys' legs are trembling like phone lines in a storm. The six gets stuck and takes a while to become five. The four is drowned out by a thunderclap.

"Three," she says. "Two . . ." Silence. My old man mouths "one" at her and waves his hand for her to go on. "O . . . O . . . One."

"Very good," my old man says and claps. "It was tough, but she did it. Now I want to hear you guys." They both shake their heads. Eyebrows bites his lips. Samuel takes a breath. "Do I really have to do it, *chamigos*?"

"Let me," says Alvarenga. "I want to have a little fun, too." He uses my old man's shoulder as a coat rack and hangs his shotgun there by the strap. He rolls up the sleeves of his military shirt.

Flamengo's lip is getting bigger and he rubs it. The rain bounces off the roof. Alvarenga walks between the two guys and over to one of the circular saws. He waves me over to help him take off the tree trunk sitting on the iron bed with tracks that go straight to the saw. When we drop it, a cloud of sawdust flies into the air. The other iron bed is empty. Ready. With our backs to them, he motions for me to go get Eyebrows, then turns and puts his arm around Flamengo.

"Back in the day, my *compadre* and I watched a lot of Bond movies, especially the Sean Connery ones. He's the only real Bond. Have you guys seen those movies?" he asks them. They both shake their heads. "I didn't think so. You didn't even exist in your dads' balls when those movies came out.

I'm going to spoil part of *Goldfinger* for you guys. We're going to do the Guaraní remake of one of the scenes."

Alvarenga punches Flamengo in the back of the neck, and he falls to the floor. Before he can react, Alvarenga has one of his feet hooked to the iron bed with a strap, then his arms. Eyebrows tries to run away, but I slam the butt of my Colt into the top of his head, and he crumples to the floor. I drag him over, and tie him to the other the iron bed, legs open, so the saw points directly at their balls.

"Whoever sings gets to go on his merry way," Alvarenga says and turns on the machine. He presses a button, and both iron tracks start to move toward the two sawblades. Twelve inches.

"Let me go, you son of a bitch," says Eyebrows.

"Those aren't the magic words."

Eight inches.

"Suck my dick!" says Flamengo, over and over. Eyebrows turns his feet inwards and shouts:

"Ñancaguazú. Ñancaguazú!"

"Your mom, too," Alvaregna says.

"Ñancaguazú River!" he shouts. "Centurión's there."

Alvarenga looks at me and stops the saws. Eyebrows starts to sob and mutter.

"On Route Twelve, past Ñancaguazu River, that's where the boss is."

"You think we should believe him?" Alvarenga asks me. "Or should I give him a little more?"

"Hit it."

"He's there. He's there," Eyebrows says, still crying. "He's got a weed plantation and a warehouse where we collect what we take across the river. He's holed up there."

"You coward. You fucking coward!" Flamengo says and spits on him. He arches his body up, telling us again to suck his dick.

My old man walks over next to me.

"Being a man of your word and being a man of honor are two different things," he says and grabs Eyebrows' hair. "I'm a man of honor."

"I swear he's there."

"I believe you." And in one movement he takes out his pistol and puts two bullets in Flamengo's face. "But there's nothing worse than a traitor. All yours," my old man says.

"I told you." Eyebrows sobs. "I told you."

I squat down next to him. A tear comes out of his eye clean and turns to mud as it runs down his face.

"I'm sorry, but you're right," I say. "The people who come along with me don't make it in one piece." And I press the button.

The saw eats up his body and spits out waves of blood to the side like a fountain. Eyebrows shrieks, and the metal teeth swallow his flesh and his screams. By the time the saw is halfway up his belly, his mouth doesn't open anymore. He ends up split in half like a *chorizo mariposa*. Each half falls to the floor and his guts spill all over the floor. The girl throws up on the floor. Alvarenga looks at my old man and bobs his head in the girl's direction.

"I'll take care of her," my old man yells over the sounds of the saws. "Come on, honey. Let's get some air."

"What's he going to do?" I ask Alvarenga, who doesn't hear me or pretends not to.

Behind me, the night lights up in a flash. He turns off the machine, and a lonely gut falls like creeping vines across the metal bars. I can't hear either my father or the girl. No. He is not going to "take care" of her with a bullet. He would have just shot her here. It's a little too late for him to save face in front of me, and he knows better. But I cannot shake that idea away.

Another flash of lighting outside. The saw, big and red, looks at me like a giant eye, giving me a blank stare that says the only way out is death. I can't handle any more blood. I start walking toward my father when I hear a shot. I don't have time to say "son of a bitch" before I hear two more shots, and I realize that my old man wasn't the one pulling the trigger.

The flash wasn't lightning—it was the highbeams of the white Isuzu that has pulled up outside. Two guys jump out of the cab, guns ready.

# 25.

"Goddamn it," Alvarenga says.

My old man comes back in alone and dives to the floor. The hammering of an automatic rifle draws a line of dots in the metal wall at stomach height. Samuel crawls behind a wall of tree trunks. He takes Alvarenga's shotgun off his shoulder and aims at the door.

Alvarenga and I crouch and get behind another pile of trunks. The Isuzu's high beams flood in the shed and cut it in half. I can feel the dust floating in the air stick to my sweaty skin. Our clothes are coated in sawdust. My old man peeks up and fires. One blast of buckshot, then another that smashes into the metal. There's a dull sound. Something leans against the holes and darkens them. Lines of blood flow down the interior surface.

"One down," Samuel says.

"How many are there?"

I can hear shots from both sides that tear bark off the

trunks. My old man's talking, but I can't hear anything over the clatter of the guns and the rain. We can hear him only when there's a pause in the shooting.

"We'll count them when they're dead."

He circles around the tree trunks and hugs the metal sheeting of the front wall. Alvarenga and I lean out and fire without aiming. All I can see is darkness. They return fire, and we take cover again. One of the trunks slips and rolls to the floor. The others follow it in a cascade that disintegrates our cover. We run to where my old man was hiding moments ago.

Someone walks in front of the Isuzu's lights, and his shadow stretches across the floor. Another one follows him, and they come inside the warehouse. My old man gives the first one a warm welcome with the shotgun, which tears off a piece of his stomach. His blood soaks the man running in behind him, blinding him. He brings his left hand up to wipe his face, and fires aimlessly with his right. The blast of buckshot from my old man's shotgun buries his hand in his face, and his fingers, nose, and mouth melt into one mess. Samuel runs over and joins us. He's breathing through his mouth, and there's sweat pouring down his face. He reloads the Ithaca.

The wood between us bursts into splinters. The bulb overhead explodes. My old man grabs me by the neck and pushes me down to the floor. Through the back door, I can see a fat guy shooting at us with a pistol, and behind him

Sherman, shotgun in hand, and another guy with an automatic. On our bellies, we take cover between the tree trunks and the wall. I look to the other side. All I can see is the rain in the headlights of the Isuzu.

"What do we do?" Alvarenga says.

My old man signals for one of us to go out to the right side of the pile of trunks and the other to the left. We do it. They try to surround us. On Alvarenga and Samuel's side, Sherman and the guy with the automatic let loose. On my side, the fat guy keeps grinding away at the trunks that shield me. I shoot at him, and the bullets strike sparks from the circular saw he's hiding behind. I crouch down. I try to stay calm, but the Colt feels like it's electrified in my hands. Alvarenga leans out and pulls the trigger. The guy's chest eats the bullet and he falls dead on a pile of beams. At the back, my old man runs Sherman out, and I lose sight of him through the door.

I wipe the sweat off my brow. The fat man and I lean out to shoot at the same time. He comes at me but steps in the ground-up flesh of Eyebrows and slips. His face bangs straight into the cutting edge of one of the saws, and he lands on the floor. I don't hesitate. I come running out. I see him on the ground, writhing around in the remains of the Paraguayan, clutching a wound that divides his face in two. I pull the trigger and blast it away.

Alvarenga reloads. I drop the empty clip of the Colt and grab a new one. My old man comes in the back door. His face changes. He pulls out his 9mm. I lift my head, and the clip falls from my hands. Two shadows are cut out against the headlights of the Isuzu, and the shed gets darker.

"Look out behind you," Alvarenga yells, and I dive behind the bandsaws.

Gamarra appears in the front door holding an FAL rifle. The lights and flashes blind me. Bursts that blink the world on and off. My hand gropes around looking for the clip. I find it. Alvarenga fires. I can't get it in. The FAL fires as if spitting out stars in the darkest night, and that night becomes suddenly darker as I see Alvarenga shake and two lines of blood spurt from his chest. My old man shouts. His gun goes quiet. He runs over to his buddy's side and drags him to cover. I load the Colt. I fire as I walk backwards and join my old man and Alvarenga. Samuel takes off Alvarenga's shirt, and I can see two red buttons on his chest that are growing.

"It's nothing," Alvarenga says. "Just bug bites."

Samuel tears off a strip of cloth and presses it against the wounds.

"Hold this," he tells me, and as soon as I put my hand down, he takes his away. He doesn't even look at me. He takes the Colt from me.

"Stop," I say. "Stop."

But there's no point. He faces them like a storm.

Sherman leans out, and Samuel fires until Centurión's son falls backwards and lets out a moan of pain. My old man goes out of the warehouse, and I lose sight of him. Holes appear in the metal siding, and the interior is filled with cords of light. It looks like a harp. Alvarenga reaches over and opens the cylinder of his .38. He reloads it, then puts his free hand on top of mine. The shirt squelches like a wet sponge, and when he squeezes it, blood leaks out. He gives me two pats on the fingers, leaving the gun in my hand.

"Go on," he says. "Go take care of him."

I hesitate. I stand up, then hesitate again. Alvarenga nods, and I run outside. The shots and rain feel closer. My old man is standing in the middle of the field, firing without even trying to take cover. Gamarra leans Sherman against the white Isuzu, and he leaves a red stain on the passenger door. He opens the door and uses it as a shield. I blast away the windows. Gamarra finishes shoving Sherman inside and starts to go around the truck shooting his FAL over the cab. The rain has washed the red stain away. My old man keeps firing the Colt, and when he's out, he takes the shotgun off his shoulder. I pull the trigger. The Isuzu turns, and my last shot goes wide. Samuel runs after it and stops to shoot. One of the taillights explodes and hangs like an eyeball torn from its socket. The bags of marijuana start to fall from the back of the truck one after the other. The Isuzu disappears down the road. Samuel throws the shotgun and runs into the shed.

The bulb at the back is the only source of light. We can see the pool of blood first, then the piece of shirt on the floor, the open first pocket of the fanny pack, and the empty eyes staring at the last cigarette between his fingers, which he didn't manage to light.

My old man doesn't say a word. He can't take his eyes off his buddy. His breath comes in pants. He closes Alvarenga's eyes, then takes the cigarette from his hand and zips up the pocket. When he stands up, he closes his eyes and reaches for his left shoulder blade, wincing in pain. He stumbles and leans against the wooden beams. I move toward him and reach him just in time to catch him as he falls. He takes off his shirt using just his right hand. He has a bullet wound in his back, but his chest is clean, no exit wound. He goes pale and tries to spit, but his mouth is too dry.

"Goddamn it," he says. "God fucking damn it."

If the bullet shattered and is moving through his veins, he won't live to tell the tale. My old man drops to one knee on the floor. He looks up at me. What I wanted for so many years could happen at any moment.

But I still need him, the way you need an amputation to survive.

I reach out and help him up. I put his arm around my neck and start to carry him to the Fairlane. With each step we take, his wound spurts blood, bathing my fingers.

"Don't die, you son of a bitch," I tell him. "Not yet."

# 26.

The rain beats against the roof and feeds the reddish puddles that form on the ground. It looks like the sky slit its wrists and is bleeding out on top of us.

My old man's back is a map of scars crossed by a red river that flows down from his shoulder. I rinse the blade of my knife in whiskey, and what's left of Anyelén's blood is washed away.

My old man takes a swig from the bottle and leaves it on the table next to Alvarenga's cigarette, the guns, my shirt, and the tackle box that serves as a first aid kit. I put a little hydrogen peroxide on the wound. It bubbles, and I wipe it away. The blade of the knife pushes into the pale and sweaty skin. Samuel bites back a moan. I dig around. The wound spits out blood that drips and pools in the waist of his jeans. I twist the blade. The plastic tablecloth wrinkles between his fingers, and when the knife touches the bullet, he jerks and the bottle smashes on the floor. I open up the flesh and twist the blade in a circle. I can feel the bullet screwed into the bone. The image of Anyelén dead flashes in front of my eyes, and my hand shakes. I scrape and break it free. The wound vomits, and the red river on his back flows stronger. I put in the pliers. I pinch them, find the bullet, take it out, and leave it on the table. My old man's fingers relax. He lets a hurricane out of his mouth and rests his forehead on the tablecloth.

"Thanks, *pichón*."

I take a needle out of the tackle box and hold it in the flame of the kitchen burner. The thread is covered in dust, and I wipe it clean with a cloth. I put a little alcohol on his back and press gauze against the hole. It's not bleeding as much now. I thread the needle and the memory of Seba coming home for me to knit him a new eyebrow surfaces somewhere in my head. I wonder if he was coming back that time from something as rough as what we just went through, if I'll ever hear stories about him, and most of all, if he's okay in jail. The rain beats on the roof. I sink the needle into my old man's flesh.

"Fuck," he says, and punches the table.

"Don't be a pussy. It's not like I'm putting in a fishing hook."

My old man laughs, and I erase his smile as I go back to embroidering his skin.

"You should be used to it by now," I say. A little worm of broken skin sits next to his spine. And that's the neatest of his scars. "If you want a little advice, next time you get shot, go get stitched up by a doctor instead of a butcher."

"Are you saying you want to do this again sometime?"

"I'm not a doctor."

"But you could have been. You had good grades."

"Do you want me to congratulate you for checking up on how I did at college?" I push in the needle angrily, and my old man's shoulder jumps. "It's a little late for what could have been."

Through the window, Samuel looks at the Fairline with the front doors open.

"You're right," he says. "About that. And about Alvarenga being more of a butcher than a doctor."

"If you're about to tell me a story of how he saved your life, you can skip it."

"I bet you weren't voted Best Personality in school, huh?"

The blood fills the wound, and I can't see where to put the needle in. I pour on some more alcohol. My old man picks up the crushed bullet and rolls it between his fingers.

"If you'd stayed here, I don't think you would've won Best Personality, either. You never know when to keep your mouth shut. But a least you would have gone to some student festivals." Without the fear that the bullet might be moving through his bloodstream, Samuel starts to loosen up. "That's where I got the first of all those scars. Alvarenga and I went to check out the girls and see if we could get any. A few parades went by before I saw her. She was

258 • NICOLÁS FERRARO

wearing this sequin dress that just sparkled, but what really blinded you were her eyes. That was the second time I saw your mother."

"Are we almost to the part where everything goes to shit? All your stories end the same."

"We went to wait for her at the bar," he goes on like I haven't said anything. "By the time she got there, we were shit-faced. She came right up to me, so I thought it'd be easy. But there were a few guys after your mom, one in particular who thought he had it in the bag. A tough little fuck. His friends were no push-overs, either. I could have just left, but I took one look at your mom and knew there was nothing they could do to scare me away."

"Are you sure you didn't get fucked in the ass in jail?"

My old man laughs again.

"I'm sure," he says. "So this guy comes over to claim what's his. I just head-butted him, knocked him clean on his ass. But there were too many of those fuckers. One of them broke a beer bottle and stabbed me in the back. I pulled it out and gave it right back to him. Alvarenga was Muhammed Ali that night. When it came to fistfights, he was an animal. When we had to go home so he could stitch up my back, you should have seen him with the needle. It was like he had Parkinson's. He ended up fucking me up worse than the kid with the beer bottle." I push the needle in for another stitch, and he yells. "You're stitching too close. The next one should be a little farther from the wound."

I huff and keep stitching however I want. I let him keep talking. They're a eulogy at a funeral no one's going to attend.

"That night I went to see your mother, and Alvarenga was right: the bigger the scar, the better the sympathy. I was out of my mind for her. Those scars are nothing compared to the damage she ended up doing to me. And every time, Alvarenga was there to cheer me up with a Negroni and a hug. You've got it all wrong, you know. Your friends don't have to save your life. They make life worth living."

He stops talking and I keep stitching. The needle pulls at the skin that's gone red around the wound like a rash.

"And kids don't make it worth living?"

"I just lost my best friend for my kids, so you do the math." He pauses. "I wasn't a good father. I didn't care much about it most of the time. But there's a reason we went to Buenos Aires. I wanted to see if I could leave this shit behind. For a while there I was snorting more than I was eating, but when they put me away living without coke was a walk in the park. But in Buenos Aires I got tempted by the life again. Some drugs are harder to quit than others. Just ask your brother. He tried it too, and he liked it. But I don't see you too angry at him."

"He tried it because you were his first dealer."

"You are what you are. You can't get away from yourself. Your mom liked to start trouble more than I liked to sort it out. And you and me are shrapnel from the same grenade. You've got the same anger in you, a compass that doesn't point the way, and if you don't know where to go, every road is just a way out. I buried my nose in gunpowder so I wouldn't have to see it, until that was the only thing I cared about. And you just let your life go by."

"If there was nobody to point the way at home, it was because you got yourself locked up."

"Yeah, you're right. But at some point it stops being the father's fault, and that's just an excuse. If you can't let go of that, you'll never do shit. Almost thirty years, and all you've got is an excuse."

He tries to turn his head to look at me.

"Stay still," I say and hurry to finish the last few stitches, as if I could trap those words inside him. I pick up a pair of scissors and cut the thread. I dig around in the first aid kit until I find some gauze and bandages.

"That saying about you not choosing your family is bullshit," says my old man, staring at the crushed bullet still between his fingers. "The most important family is the one that you make with the people you want. Ours . . . well, you know. I'm not here to redeem your father, just your brother. You can write the whole dad thing down on the list of things that could have been." He puts the bullet down on the table and looks at me. "But it's like everything in your life is already on that list."

"If you're done playing father of the year, shut your trap and let me finish patching you up."

My old man gives a tired smile that fades on his face,

then disappears. I press the gauze against the wound and start to wrap the bandage under his armpit and across the space between his neck and shoulder so he can still move. So he can reload. That's what my old man is. A gun. Something that's better left in a wooden box when it isn't shooting.

Samuel moves his arm and stifles a groan.

"Pretty good," he says.

"Now what?"

"Centurión's been looking for me for years. Now I'm going to give him the pleasure of meeting me."

"He's going to be waiting for us with Gamarra and the whole crew."

"Good."

He stands up. His first steps are gingerly and he leans on the table, then he lets go and heads for the shed. He comes out soaking wet from the rain, with a shovel in his hand.

"You're going to pull all your stitches out," I yell. "That can wait."

My old man shakes his head and pushes the shovel into the soft ground in the middle of the yard. Once. Twice. Three times. A little mountain starts to grow next to his feet, and a red spot appears on his bandage.

"You fucking son of bitch," I say.

I get another shovel from a hook in the shed and stand in front of him. I start to dig. The rain beats on our backs, and the lightning dyes the sky blue. We dig, two holes that separate us, then a bit more and the holes become a single pit that brings us together. We give life to a grave.

The first thing my old man and I have made together.

I don't know if we've ever been closer. I don't think we'll ever be this close again. And I laugh. And he laughs. I stop feeling the drops on my back and the sweat on my face, and I dig. He turns to one side, and I can see the bandage is completely red. My old man didn't shed a single tear for his friend, but he's bleeding for him. I sink the shovel into the ground and unearth a part of Samuel I'd never seen before. My old man might be a weapon, but he'll blast away with everything he has for his own.

"That's good," he says, looking at the hole.

We open the back doors of the Fairlane. Samuel drags out Alvarenga's body and lets me get his legs. He doesn't even look when he grabs the arms. The body's heavy. It's not stiff yet. I think about Anyelén, about what might have happened to what was left of her, about the fact that it doesn't matter anymore. We put Alvarenga in the hole as gently as if we were setting a baby down in a cradle. We cover him up. The red mud eats him up little by little until it finally swallows him completely.

My old man stands staring at that pile of disturbed earth, bent over, his hands gripping the handle of the shovel. He hangs his head between his shoulders, and his face screws up in a grimace of pain. I leave him alone.

A few minutes go by before he comes back. He walks in

pulling off the bandage, and I've already got a new one ready to put on him. The stitches have held. As soon as I wrap him up, he goes into a bedroom and comes back with a plaid shirt on and a bag full of boxes of bullets. He hands me a couple of clips for the Colt and I put a new one in as he loads the sawed-off, Alvarenga's .38, and the Browning 9mm.

We sit at the table, face to face under a yellow light that does more to stretch out our shadows than illuminate us. My old man picks up Alvarenga's cigarette and lights it with his Zippo. He takes a drag, then lets the smoke out slowly. Gathered in his mouth, it looks like rabies froth. He holds the cigarette out to me. I haven't smoked since I was fifteen, but I reach out and take it. I give it a long drag and stifle a cough. It's so quiet, I can hear the paper and tobacco burning. I hand it back to him, and we pass it back and forth until my old man takes the last drag. When he puts it out, I realize how much light an ember can give off.

"I've got something for you," I say. "I thought about giving it to you a few times, but never like this."

"You're going to get blood on you if you try to give me a hug now, *pichón*."

I shake my head. I reach into my pocket and take it out.

"Gamarra gave it to Seba's daughter." I put the bullet on the table. "You're going to do a better job of giving it back to him than I am."

My old man picks up the 9mm bullet between his forefinger and thumb. He grabs the Browning and cocks out the round in the chamber. He pulls out the clip and pushes in the bullet I just gave him. He cocks the gun and puts it in his waistband. Now only Anyelén's necklace deforms Seba's picture in my wallet. I rub my finger across it and feel the links in the chain. This is the closest to praying I've ever come. Samuel comes around the table, and I hurry to close my wallet. He puts his hand on my shoulder and says:

"They wanted to bury us." He grabs the sawed-off and slings it over his shoulder. "But they forgot we're seeds."

# 27.

There's nothing but a black smear above us, like God covered over the cadaver of the sky with a sheet. It seems like we're the last thing left in the world.

My old man, sitting on the hood of the Fairlane, pets the sawed-off like a dog. The look in his eyes makes me think the storm is trapped inside him.

"Let's go," he says.

We walk blind, following the Ñancaguazú and feeling our way through the trees. The river is flowing fast, just like the blood in my veins, when the pine trees disappear and we see in front of us a forest of weed surrounding a huge abandoned structure. The lightbulbs here and there illuminate patches of the two-story building made of old bricks and rusty corrugated iron. The wooden beams and doors are eaten by moss, and the glass in the windows is spiderwebbed by the impact of bullets. At the edge of the plantation is a cabin made of rotting wood. The door is open, and a yellow stab of light shines out onto the marijuana. Farther down, I can see the broken windshield of the white Isuzu behind a building that looks like it used to be a stable.

I start forward, and my old man places the sawed-off across my chest. Then he points into the darkness with the barrel and shows me three lines of barbed wire in our way. He moves down the fence until we reach the river. As we step into the water, the current flows over our feet, and the mud swallows them up. Two steps later, we're on the other side.

The plants are chest-high. My old man hangs the sawed-off over his shoulder and moves forward with Alvarenga's .38 at the ready. We can't see movement in any of the buildings. I wonder where Centurión is. Whether my old man will survive. If we'll be able to get Seba out. What it must be like to be a father. Making a family with Alina. Whether our child would have her eyes. I want so many answers, but all I've got is the Colt in my hand and this wish not to die so I can find them.

When we reach the edge of the plantation, my old man waves for me to stop. He takes two steps, and as he takes the sawed-off from his shoulder, he puts his back to the wall of the cabin. He starts to move around it, and I lose sight of him. I can hear someone swearing from inside. I step out of the plants and see the flash of the shotgun light up the field through the open shutter. Another flash. By the time I make it to the door, Samuel is reloading the shotgun. It's hard to believe that the steaming pile of meat strewn across the floor and walls was a person two buckshot ago.

We hear shouting from inside, and I see lights come on through the window. My old man jerks his head for me to follow him. He goes into the stable, but there are only bags of marijuana.

He doesn't have to tell me this time. As we pass by the white Isuzu, I slash the tires.

"Good," says my old man as we kneel down next to the truck. Sherman's not around, but there's about a quart of his blood in the passenger seat. We go around the side and find another entrance to the building. The metal door is open, and there's a red handprint on it. Samuel rubs his shoulder and grimaces. He runs to the door, and I follow him, ignoring the red stain on the side of the Isuzu that might have come from Sherman or my old man.

We move into the darkness inside the building. Our breathing echoes in the silence. I can taste earth and damp in my mouth. Shouting and shots in the distance. There's so little light coming in that if it were coke, you wouldn't be able to scrape together a line. I move forward with my back to the wall. My hands and forehead are sweaty. A few yards on, I find a line of light that grows across the floor and climbs up the wall. Through the windows, we see two men run by to surround us. Samuel signals for me to keep going, and he leans against the wall, aiming for the door.

I push the door with the barrel of the Colt and see a

hallway with a construction lamp hanging from a cable. There's a trail of blood that disappears behind another metal door. I kick it in. I sweep my gun left and right across what might be used as an office. Two chairs face each other across a metal desk, and the windows are filled in with bricks. Someone counted down the days with chalk on the wall next to a pair of chains that end in handcuffs. On the floor are women's clothes and broken dolls. There's a mattress made of cardboard boxes and potato chip bags. A pair of ruffly little girls' underwear next to dirty diapers. The flies buzz between those and used condoms. Farther back, a broken baby bottle, the sharp glass stained red. Only in this hell could a baby bottle be a weapon. I wonder if she used it to cut someone else or herself.

Sons of bitches.

I don't have any more time to wonder because a door on the other side of the room opens. It's the fat guy who was loading up bricks with Eyebrows. He's got a double-barrel in his hands pointed straight at me. I dive behind the desk. The first scattering of buckshot rattles the drawers, and the next one spits them to the floor. I lean out to fire, but he jumps on me, using the shotgun as a club, landing it right in my chest. We hit the floor. The pistol falls from my hand, and he presses the shotgun down on my throat. I manage to get my left hand in above my Adam's apple before he can crush it. I reach with my right hand, but the Colt seems a whole lifetime away. I try to get my knife, but the fat guy's legs are covering the sheath. I cough and spit. The shotgun bears down on me, a metal collar that's becoming a noose as my lungs struggle for air. This is hell, I tell myself. And I reach out again, grab the broken baby bottle, and bury it in his side. He lets go of me for a second, long enough for me to reach the Colt. He jumps back on top of me and tries to get the pistol. The shot tears his neck apart. A spurt of blood splashes the lightbulb, and the whole room goes red. He tries to staunch the bleeding. A second shot to the head stops him worrying about it.

In the distance, I hear the thunder of shots from my old man's sawed-off and shrieks that die with new gun blasts. I rub my neck. My throat is dry. Samuel comes in, his jeans sprinkled with blood, and looks at the dead man next to me.

"You okay?"

I point to the trail of red drops on the floor.

"Must not have much left," he says and starts to follow it like a hound.

Another hallway. Another door. Ripped panties. A few long strands of hair hanging from a nail that sticks out from the wall. The name Lila is written on a wall in lipstick, one word so that someone will remember her. The world keeps falling to pieces until my old man kicks a metal door and we step out into space. A demolished room, bricks scattered across the floor. Ten yards farther on, the building begins again. There's a door with an open grate and a window glass so dirty it looks frosted.

My old man doesn't hesitate. He moves forward with the .38 held up in one hand. A figure appears in the window. The glass explodes. The bullets bounce off the corrugated iron next to me, sparking. I jump to the side and flatten myself against the wall. My old man moves to the other side and returns fire, shattering a few windowpanes.

"Come on, you pussies," Sherman shouts. He has a red-stained bandage around his head and another across his stomach. His white-dusted nose and frenzied grin light up as his Uzi fires at us again.

Samuel and I, each on our own, huddle down behind piles of rubble. I'm at the other end of the room, diagonal from the window. My old man's directly in front of it. The whole space is filled with a mist of cement and gunpowder.

Gamarra appears next to Sherman, and when I pop at them, they duck for cover. My old man's lying face-up with the .38 on his chest like a rosary. Gamarra tries to drag Sherman out, but he shoves him away with his shoulder.

"Get out of here, Gamarra," he says. "I'll take care of that old faggot myself."

He fires again. Samuel looks at me and points to the left, then the right. I look at the window. Left, I signal him. He rolls over. Sherman keeps pulling the trigger, grinning like a madman. My old man stands up in one movement and fires. The shot destroys Sherman's shoulder. He stumbles backwards and tries to keep control of his body but ends up tumbling forward onto the spires of glass left in the windowframe. The smile on his face disappears as a shard of glass slices him a new one in his throat. His head lolls to the side and comes to rest against the windowframe. Blood starts to bubble out of his mouth and drip over our side of the window.

My old man walks forward firing, and I follow him. We plaster ourselves to the wall next to the door. He opens the cylinder of the .38. Empty. He throws it aside and grabs the sawed-off again. Sherman's body finally slips free and collapses to the floor with a thud. Gamarra fires, and he's joined by the sound of another gun shooting at us. My ears are exploding. Holes start to appear in the metal door, and it comes loose from its hinges, falling to the floor between us.

"Cruz, you son of a bitch," Centurión shouts. Whatever he says next is drowned by the sound of his automatic.

My old man looks at me and mouths the words "cover me," pointing at the window. Crouching, I shuffle over, and when he nods, I stand and fire. I see Centurión at the end of a huge room that looks like a dining area. There are four long tables, two on each side, fixed to the wall. The farthest from me on the left is covered in bricks of coke, and my old man's shots force Gamarra to duck behind the cement base of the table. Samuel runs in and hides behind the nearest table.

Crazy bastard. I don't know if he has a plan or if he just went kamikaze. I try to follow him up, but my body refuses to move. The bullets keep flying, in a loop. Here and there, little clouds of dust; the line of Sherman's blood thins as it touches ground, creating a little pond. I look at the window, waiting to see a red spray of my old man, see him jolted by bullets, his whole body twisting as his bones pile up on the floor. I will be next.

My father has made the world a dark place wherever he put his feet, but I feel that, right now, the world would be a much darker place without him, without the light of his guns blazing.

I don't like my odds if they kill him, so when the two of them shoot, I run in firing and take cover on the right. My old man stands, and his sawed-off roars, searching for Gamarra. A couple of bricks explode in a shower of white powder. Gamarra jumps up and fires. Samuel falls backwards, and his second shot hits the roof. Gamarra rushes in to execute him, but I open fire and he has to take cover again.

My old man drags himself to the edge of the table and rests his back against the cement wall. He presses his left hand to his waist. A new wound spurts blood over his fingers like brass knuckles. He cracks open the sawed-off, and his grimace disappears behind a cloud of gunsmoke. With just his right hand, he loads one shell, but the other slips out of his fingers and falls to the floor. He takes out another and finishes reloading. He pulls himself into a squat. I lean up and fire at Centurión hiding in the rubble of the room at the back. Gamarra takes aim at me, and when he pulls the trigger he realizes he's out. I get one shot off at him before I hear the click that forces me to take cover and reload.

My old man rushes out for him, but all he finds are bricks of coke. Gamarra appears on the other side of the table. With one hand, he pushes the sawed-off away, and with the other he buries a knife in Samuel's chest. Before he can stab him again, Samuel jumps on him, and they roll across the table and land on the other side. I hear them struggling. Groans. Heavy thuds.

Centurión's still firing at me, and I can't get up. The splinters of wood pile up on the floor. I duck to the other side of the room and stand. I surprise him, and my shot forces him back. The darkness swallows him up. I walk forward, shooting at the spot where he was. His automatic flashes twice before it goes hoarse.

Someone comes out from between the tables, and I take aim: it's my old man. His breathing is ragged, and he's so covered in blood it looks like he's sweating it. He stands up shakily. There's a gash across his forehead. He wipes at it with one hand, but his face is covered with a red mask again in seconds.

I can't hear any more noises coming from the back. Then a door opens in the distance and I can see marijuana plants, but no Centurión.

I go over to my old man. Gamarra's sitting on the floor leaning against the cement wall. His eyes are fixed on his right hand, pinned to his own stomach with the knife. His left hand trembles, trying to reach the handle. He raises his head and laughs.

"Tough motherfuckers are the last to die, huh?" he says.

"Only the biggest sons of bitches," my old man replies. He takes the Browning from his waistband and points it at him. "This is from my granddaughter." And he pulls the trigger. He gives him back his bullet, along with the rest of the clip. His head is eaten up bit by bit by the lead.

When he takes his finger off the trigger, Samuel sways. It looks like he's going to fall backwards, but he finally lands on top of the table covered with coke. The Browning slips from his fingers.

"*Pichón* . . . he gutted me really ugly." He puts his right hand to the cut in his chest, then to the wound at his waist. His jeans are stained like he's pissed himself, and his shirt is stuck to his skin. He takes it off, balls it up, and presses it against his waist, trying to stop the bleeding. His blood dips on the coke and turns it to a pinkish paste. "Looks like you're going to need a lot of thread."

I reload the Colt and shake my head. I help him sit on the table and lay him down, using a brick of coke as a pillow. I take off my shirt and hand it to him. It's all I have to give him.

I can kill Centurión and save Seba, or save my old man.

It's an easy decision, and he knows it.

Barely opening his mouth, he says:

"Bring me his head."

# 28.

The sun unearths itself behind the marijuana plants.

I check the grass, but I can't find a trail to follow. Farther back is another cabin that looks recently built. The reinforced door is open, and the windows look bullet-proof. A five-star bunker. Parked to one side is a burgundy Ranger with tinted glass. I look for the house's blind spot, and when I find it, I move closer.

When I'm ten yards away, I slow my pace and step forward slowly. The wind rustles the plantation. Birds are singing somewhere off in the pines. I hear a snort from inside the house.

I raise the Colt in both hands and aim at the door, still moving closer. I hear the bolt of a gun. Another sniff. Dull steps on a wood floor. As soon as a bit of air enters my lungs, I push it back out my mouth. I take one long step and shove my way in, opening fire inside the cabin. The bullets hit an empty table and bricks of coke, raising geysers of white. But they don't hit Centurión, who's nowhere to be seen.

There's an open door at the back. I check left and right and decide to head for the truck. I sweep the Colt from side to side. By the time I see his reflection in the Ranger's window, it's too late. We both jump back and open fire. The shot of the Smith & Wesson explodes next to my ear, jarring me. Bullets from the Colt smash the front and rear tinted windows. Centurión trips and falls. The last shot cuts the grass next to his boots. His face is covered in coke and sticky with sweat. I'm not sure whether to change my clip or jump on him. When he lifts his arm to aim at me, I rush him. I push his arm aside with my right hand, and the shot chips the Ranger's paint. Once. Twice. He keeps struggling, and I trap his body between my legs. With both hands, I grab his fingers wrapped around the butt of the gun and smash them against the side of the truck. He fires one more shot and when he hears a click he drops the gun. He catches me with a right hook to the liver. As I gasp for breath, he wrestles his way on top of me. Now he's got me trapped under his legs. I try to punch him, but he twists his body out of the way. He reaches for his back and pulls out another gun. The son of a bitch laughs, and the pasty white mask cracks on his face. He savors the moment. A little too much. When he raises the gun, I bury my knife in him just above his dick and start cutting. The blade moves upwards. The gun falls from his fingers, and his guts spill out on me as I open him up, until the blade hits his sternum. I pull the blade out and sink it back into his flesh.

Again and again.

And again.

I only stop when I think Anyelén would have said it was enough. There's more of Centurión on me that inside his body. There's a hole in his stomach that looks like it was made by a cannonball. I stand up and watch the bits of him slither and form a pile in the grass.

It's over, I say to myself.

It's over.

I walk back as an orange sunrise appears as the only witness and the shadows begin to disappear. This part of the day has always seemed somehow unreal to me. It's the moment that makes me wonder if what's happening is really true. You open your eyes and you don't know if you're coming out of a dream or a nightmare, or if that's reality.

Every once in a while as a kid I'd wake up and think I saw my old man standing in the doorway watching us sleep. Sometimes I heard him whispering, like he wanted to tell us something he didn't dare to say out loud. Whenever I asked if it was him standing there, Samuel said no way. But when I went back to my room, I could see the cigarette butts in the doorway.

Coming out of my memories, I'm running toward him, wondering if there's anything I can do patch up my old man.

In the warehouse, all I can see of Samuel is his blood on

the coke. I find him sprawled on the floor, smoking, surrounded by a few bricks of coke that fell during the struggle. There's a bloody bullet in his hand and a deep gash in his hip.

"It wasn't so hard," he says in a tired voice as he takes a drag on his cigarette.

I help him to his feet.

"Couldn't you just lie still?"

"I was bleeding all over the coke."

"What the hell do you care?"

He blinks a few times and when he can see me clearly, he smiles.

"Because all of this belongs to me now."

I take a step back.

"There's got to be a king, *pichón*." He shows me Gamarra's cell phone. "Di Pietro's on his way right now to give me my crown."

I push him against the table, and he grabs it for support. The balled-up shirt on his wound comes unstuck and falls to the floor.

"All of this . . . You never gave a shit about getting Seba out."

He bends down, picks up two bricks, and sets them on the table with the rest.

"You can think whatever you want, but I wasn't going to be the only dipshit left empty-handed. I promised you your brother, and you've got him."

We stare at each other for a few seconds. The cigarette

burns itself away between his fingers and goes out when it touches the blood. The smoke snakes away and disappears.

And then I walk away. In the doorway, I stop and turn around.

I want to say something. But all I have left is silence.

My old man piles up a wall made of bricks of coke and disappears behind it.

# 29.

The bars close behind my brother.

As he comes closer, his slow steps become surer, and the darkness that clouds his face comes apart like little scabs that pull away to reveal scars. A beard has swallowed up his face, but even so I can see him smile when he recognizes me sitting on the trunk of the 206.

He sighs, lifts his eyes up to the sky, and starts walking again. He stops after two steps. He looks me up and down, then closes his eyes. His lips tremble. I don't know if he's about to say something or start crying. He hugs me the way you hug someone you thought you'd lost.

We stay like that for a moment. Just like the night they took Samuel away.

"Everything's going to be okay," I say.

I wonder if my brother lied, too. He steps back, and with his hands on my shoulders, he says:

"You're here. Everything's already okay."

I nod quickly and drop my eyes to the ground. His sneakers are covered in mud and the laces are missing. His shadow stretches across the dirt and looks like it's hooked to the bars of the jail's entrance. As the clouds walk in front of the setting sun, it disappears.

"Take me home, Tommy."

I start up the 206 and the jail drops away behind us.

Beside the road are tea plantations. Perfect rows of plants. A few farms scattered around with gates that are never closed and cows, horses, and dogs that wander freely with no chains but their own lungs. I think about how free I felt the first time I saw that landscape with my brother sitting next to me and how I thought there was some meaning there, a place where we could lose who we used to be, who we didn't want to be anymore.

It's amazing how much you can lie to yourself.

Out of the corner of my eye, I see Seba's hand over his mouth like he's holding back something he wants to say. *Yes. I was with him.* I bet that would be the answer to his question. I want to look my brother straight in the face and see what's there. But neither of us look away from the road that rises and falls, from the cracks in the pavement covered in red dust.

As we come out of a curve, the sun hits our eyes. The light drives away the shadows on his face, and I can see that the dark circles under his eyes are bruises.

"What happened?" I finally ask, and regret it as soon as I remember the visits Seba was supposed to get.

My brother takes a deep breath and stops, his face partway into a wince. He touches his ribs.

"Stuff I'd rather forget," he says when he lets out his breath. He looks at the cuts and scrapes on my hand resting on the gear shift. "What about you?"

I don't know where to start, so I just reply:

"Stuff I'd rather forget."

"Whatever you've done . . . The things we do for the people we love . . ."

His words stop short, fall away.

"I heard you saw him . . ." he says a couple of miles later.

A truck with a rusted hood and a bed full of harvested plants comes toward us in the other lane. There are bits of *yerba mate* leaves littering the road.

"I'm sorry. That must have been shitty."

I cough out a laugh.

"Seeing him wasn't the worst part."

My brother looks away and rests his head against the window. In his reflection, I can see his eyes squeezed shut.

"Sometimes," he says, "I think about how things would have turned out if she had stuck around."

"Really? She never was a mother, Seba. You and I are orphans."

I wonder if this is one of those times when somebody says something to convince themselves. My brother doesn't reply. We pass the stubble of a harvested field, and the tea plantations are replaced by trees that crowd next to the road.

Seba rolls down the window and stretches his neck. The air whips at his hair, tinted orange by the sun. He takes a deep breath, lets it out, and brings his head back inside the window.

"Are you okay?" I ask.

"No," he says. "You?"

"Me neither."

I let my eyes pass over everything around us. The trees become shadows and melt together into one forest. The birds become one flock. The earth and the sky share the same red and are the same thing. Just like my brother and me. I feel like I can keep driving and reach the sky and then everything will be okay.

The sun goes down and the darkness separates the world across the horizon, and I know there are certain things you can't survive.

I speed up and don't bother braking or talking anymore until we get to my brother's house. The Di Pietro security car that brought Viviana and Lelé back stood guard for a while, but it's been gone for days now.

Seba looks at his house, the only one with Christmas decorations still up. Inside, the lights on the tree twinkle and shine on the overgrown grass in the front yard.

"I promised Lelé we'd open up presents together," he says and gets out. "Are you coming in?"

I walk around the front of the 206. A light comes on in the front window.

"I've got to take care of a few things first," I say.

He stares at me.

"Tommy . . . you and me . . . we . . ."

"Don't worry about it, brother." I'm the one who hugs him.

When I start the car, the front door of the house opens and Viviana and Lelé come running out to hug him.

This is the first promise I've ever kept in my whole life.

Now it's time to keep the second one.

# 30.

You could say a lot of things about Samuel and Alvarenga, but you couldn't deny that when one of them promised you something, he came through.

The problem was that they almost never made promises.

I got the call two days before they let my brother out. The guy, who said his name was Craviotto, was talking on behalf of Alvarenga and wanted to meet with me.

The next morning, we met at the ÑanduTi bar. He arrived late and had a Chivas Regal for breakfast as he turned the pages of a newspaper. Senator Di Pietro announced that a large drug trafficking ring had been dismantled.

"Goddamn shame what happened to Alvarenga," Craviotto said after folding up the newspaper, just before ordering a second Chivas. "We should be worried, kid. A world where your old man and Alvarenga can die is a dangerous world."

I told him to get on with it. He laughed.

"You're definitely a Cruz."

288 • NICOLÁS FERRARO

He started rattling off information.

The best and worst things in life start with a promise.

"It was always the same story. Centurión and his crew had promised Anyelén's sister, Laura, a job as a nanny in Buenos Aires. They went through the motions at first, then kidnapped her, raped her, and kept her doped up. They opened her up and put the fear in her. If she talked, her whole family would be coming along to keep her company. She'd be taking care of any man that had money to pay, but no kids. The only kids she took care of were the raw ones she could swallow. Up until they changed the menu on her. None of the girls thought about opening their mouths to say something, only to swallow a condom full of drugs and say, 'Please, sir, I want some more.'"

Then they'd send them off to Europe, pregnant with coke, along with a few others so they'd look like a family. Families aren't suspicious. Then on one of the trips the drop-off went south and Laura had to escape on her own. She was missing for two weeks. I can imagine Gamarra knocking on Anyelén's door.

By the time she made it back, she found the house empty and all she could think to do was go to the police.

"She told them everything she knew, including a couple of places where Centurión had his whorehouses. 'Please find my sister' are the last words she managed in her statement before she had a panic attack. They told her to calm down and took her to the bathroom. Who knows what she thought, maybe she was paranoid they were all in bed with Centurión. Anyway, she ran off and never showed up again at the address she'd given them.

"Your brother landed in jail the next day, and they had someone new to pick on. And that girl was good at hide and seek. It took me a few days to pick up her trail, and I had to leave a lot of bait lying around. I knew she must have left word with her neighbors in case her little sister showed up.

"You give them a little something to snort and then they feel like being talkative. I had to talk to a lot of stubborn people." He rubbed his first two fingers and his thumb together. "But I found her."

I handed him a roll of bills. He had to look through four pockets of his old suit before he found the slip of paper. I asked him to translate his scribbles and wrote the address down on a napkin.

NOW I HAVE THE napkin in my hand and the address matches the one I parked at, where Posadas starts to disintegrate.

Laura exchanged desperation for tragedy. They turned her body into a garbage bag that they ripped up and threw pieces of her into the street. And now I have to tell her that her sister is dead.

The little house mixes old wood with peeling paint with new boards waiting for their first coat. There's a window

290 • NICOLÁS FERRARO

with a ripped screen, and the left wall is made of a broken kiddie pool. Next to the door, the numbers painted in white run down the wood as if they were candles.

Hope and torture are the same word. Two different ways to suffer.

I put my hand in my pocket and touch the chain in my wallet to make sure it's still there, protected by the picture of my brother. I swallow, and my mouth is dry. The napkin with the address on it is a crumpled ball in my hand. I knock once so gently that it doesn't even make noise, then again, harder. My hands are shaking so much I drop the napkin. A dog barks and jumps on the neighbor's plot.

I want to go home, but I stay for Anyelén.

I can hear scraping footfalls inside. There's no peephole in the door, but there are a few bits of wood missing.

"Laura?"

She opens up a couple of inches. Her hair falls from behind her ear and covers the half of her face not hidden in the shadows. A few beams of light come in through the holes in the kiddie pool, and I can see that the floor is dirt.

"Who is it?"

A horse-drawn cart dragging recyclables rattles by. The dog barks at the horse.

"Centurión's dead," I say.

"Dead?" she asks, opening the door a little more.

She looks a lot like Anyelén. Her light green eyes move side to side like those of a trapped animal. She's barefoot, and the T-shirt she's wearing is so big on her it looks like a dress.

"Everyone who hurt you is dead," I tell her, as if I'm talking to my own daughter.

Her hands scrunch up the T-shirt, and when she lets it go she bites her lips.

"Your sister . . . Anyelén . . ."

I put my right hand into my pocket, and she moves to close the door. If my mouth wasn't bone dry, I'd tell her not to worry. I show her the wallet so she sees I don't have a gun. I open it and start to pull out the chain. She takes a step back as if I really had taken out a gun. I hold the chain out to her, dangling between my fingers.

"She . . ." I begin.

Laura's face changes, and I realize she's not looking at the chain, but something closer to me. Her sadness mixes with rage in her eyebrows and mouth, and her skin wrinkles.

"Is he dead, too?"

She points at the picture of my brother.

"What is it?"

The chain falls from my hand and curls up like a snake on the ground.

"That's . . ." she says. "That's the piece of shit who kid-napped me."

# 31.

Family is the worst trap.

Shared blood disguises lies.

Especially the ones that are the hardest to believe.

*Your brother's job*, that's what Centurión said.

The words were always there. Dangling liked hanged men still kicking.

When I wake up the next day I see the beer cans strewn across the table and the floor. The Colt is lying there, and my knife is out of its sheath. At some point in the night I stabbed the cans and made little crosses out of the aluminum and put them in a pile.

And in the middle of it all, something explodes in my brain, something I never thought I'd say: my old man isn't the biggest son of a bitch in the Cruz family.

I grab the car keys, the Colt, and the knife and head out.

———

**THE HOUSE ISN'T DECORATED** anymore, and the grass has been cut. On the other side of the fence around the patio, Oli barks and wags her tail when I get out of the car.

Sometimes a father is just someone who fucked the woman who gave birth to you, and a brother is just a birth control pill she forgot to take, a chain she thought would keep him from leaving. A chain. Yeah. That's the right word.

I knock.

"Tommy," Sebastián says with a smile.

He moves aside so I can come inside, but when I don't take a step, he leans against the door frame facing me. We look at each other. He isn't smiling anymore.

"Tommy," he says in a voice that seems to come up from the bottom of a well.

He swallows.

He knows I know.

He steps back but doesn't manage to dodge my fist. I feel his nose break against my knuckles and his lip splitting open against his teeth. He tries to get away and trips over an end table. A vase breaks on the floor. He lands on his ass and touches his nose. It's spurting blood and splits his face in half like two pieces of a broken mask.

He wipes his face with his T-shirt and I can see the finger-shaped stains. My shadow settles over him. He curls up to protect himself from a second blow.

"Tommy," he says, spitting out the blood that collects on his lips.

The words I'm looking for don't exist, and if they did, they wouldn't do any good. So I turn and walk away. The click of high heels rushes toward us.

"What happened?" Viviana says, trying to lift up her husband, who doesn't say anything. "What did you do, Tomás? What the fuck did you do?"

When I get into the car, Lelé comes running out. She jumps and dodges her parents' arms. "Uncle Tommy," she shouts.

I open my wallet, take out the picture of my brother, and throw it out the window. It swoops like a dry leaf and lands next to Lelé's sneakers. She picks it up, holds out her hand, and gives it back to me.

I drive off.

In the rearview mirror I see a beautiful little girl who isn't my niece anymore.


**I FINALLY BRAKE I** don't know how many blocks later. I screw my eyes shut to keep any tears from falling. My eyelids fuse together like a scar. I can barely breathe, so I roll down the window, take a breath, sigh. I close my eyes again. I tame my anger like a horse. I open my eyes and look at my split knuckles.

The last thing my brother gave me was a wound.

Samuel was right.

The family that matters is the one you choose yourself.

I lean up in my seat and take out my wallet again. Where the picture of Seba was, piled on top of each other, are the pictures of Alina. Worn and faded. There are five coins in my other pocket. I get out and feed them into a payphone. The sun is high in the sky, and I don't cast a shadow.

I dial.

When I hear her voice I can see my smile growing in my reflection in the window.

"Hey, Alina. I'm on my way."

# ACKNOWLEDGMENTS

I wrote this book almost eight years ago. At the moment, I'd written five novels and none of them was close to being published. I was determined to make this one count. The fact that you are reading this is far beyond my expectations. But I wouldn't have been able to do it without a lot of people. I owe a debt of gratitude to everyone who was there with me.

Thanks:

To Leo Oyola and his crew, with whom I worked on this novel.

To my parents, for trusting and supporting me each step of the way.

To my grandparents, especially to my nona, Edi, my first listener/reader. Perdón, Nona, for all the bad words.

To Lila and Jazz, my cats, for the company while I'm writing.

To Mallory, for dealing with my savage Spanish and making it out alive.

To the writers who cover my back with their words:

Horacio Convertini, Gabriela Cabezón Cámara, Claudio Cerdán, Juan Mattio, Guillermo Orsi y Kike Ferrari.

To Iñigo Amonarriz, my editor in Argentina, who decided to bet on *Cruz* before anyone else, and who was in the trenches with me side by side. And still is.

To el Jefe Mauricio Bares and la Jefa Lilia Barajas who gave *Cruz* an opportunity in Mexico, and to Marc Moreno, who published it in Spain.

To Jim Sallis, the first one to read *Cruz* in English and whose words and support I'll always cherish.

To Tom Wickersham, who encouraged me to give a shot to *Cruz* in the US. And for finding a great home for the book. You nailed it!

To Juliet Grames, Yezanira Venecia, Taz Urnov, and the whole Soho team, for the opportunity and all the work, patience and love they put into this book to make it better.

To Damián Vives, Mariano Sánchez, Ariel Mazzeo and Mariano Pettinati, my personal Dream Team. Much love to these ones. Without them, I wouldn't be the writer, much less the person, I am today.

# Other Titles in the Soho Crime Series

**STEPHANIE BARRON**
(Jane Austen's England)
*Jane and the Twelve Days
   of Christmas
Jane and the Waterloo Map
Jane and the Year Without a
   Summer
Jane and the Final Mystery*

**F.H. BATACAN**
(Philippines)
*Smaller and Smaller Circles*

**JAMES R. BENN**
(World War II Europe)
*Billy Boyle
The First Wave
Blood Alone
Evil for Evil
Rag & Bone
A Mortal Terror
Death's Door
A Blind Goddess
The Rest Is Silence
The White Ghost
Blue Madonna
The Devouring
Solemn Graves
When Hell Struck Twelve
The Red Horse
Road of Bones
From the Shadows
Proud Sorrows*

*The Refusal Camp: Stories*

**KATE BEUTNER**
(Massachusetts)
*Killingly*

**CARA BLACK**
(Paris, France)
*Murder in the Marais
Murder in Belleville
Murder in the Sentier
Murder in the Bastille
Murder in Clichy
Murder in Montmartre
Murder on the Ile Saint-Louis
Murder in the Rue de Paradis
Murder in the Latin Quarter
Murder in the Palais Royal*

**CARA BLACK CONT.**
*Murder in Passy
Murder at the Lanterne Rouge
Murder Below Montparnasse
Murder in Pigalle
Murder on the Champ de Mars
Murder on the Quai
Murder in Saint-Germain
Murder on the Left Bank
Murder in Bel-Air
Murder at the Porte de Versailles*

*Three Hours in Paris
Night Flight to Paris*

**HENRY CHANG**
(Chinatown)
*Chinatown Beat
Year of the Dog
Red Jade
Death Money
Lucky*

**BARBARA CLEVERLY**
(England)
*The Last Kashmiri Rose
Strange Images of Death
The Blood Royal
Not My Blood
A Spider in the Cup
Enter Pale Death
Diana's Altar*

*Fall of Angels
Invitation to Die*

**COLIN COTTERILL**
(Laos)
*The Coroner's Lunch
Thirty-Three Teeth
Disco for the Departed
Anarchy and Old Dogs
Curse of the Pogo Stick
The Merry Misogynist
Love Songs from a Shallow Grave
Slash and Burn
The Woman Who Wouldn't Die
Six and a Half Deadly Sins
I Shot the Buddha
The Rat Catchers' Olympics
Don't Eat Me
The Second Biggest Nothing*

**COLIN COTTERILL CONT.**
*The Delightful Life of
   a Suicide Pilot*

*The Motion Picture Teller*

**ELI CRANOR**
(Arkansas)
*Don't Know Tough
Ozark Dogs*

**MARIA ROSA CUTRUFELLI**
(Italy)
*Tina, Mafia Soldier*

**TERESA DOVALPAGE**
(Cuba)
*Death Comes in through
   the Kitchen
Queen of Bones
Death under the Perseids*

*Death of a Telenovela Star
   (A Novella)*

**DAVID DOWNING**
(World War II Germany)
*Zoo Station
Silesian Station
Stettin Station
Potsdam Station
Lehrter Station
Masaryk Station
Wedding Station*

(World War I)
*Jack of Spies
One Man's Flag
Lenin's Roller Coaster
The Dark Clouds Shining*

*Diary of a Dead Man on Leave*

**RAMONA EMERSON**
(Navajo Nation)
*Shutter*

**NICOLÁS FERRARO**
(Argentina)
*Cruz*

**AGNETE FRIIS**
(Denmark)
*What My Body Remembers
The Summer of Ellen*

**TIMOTHY HALLINAN**
(Thailand)
*The Fear Artist*
*For the Dead*
*The Hot Countries*
*Fools' River*
*Street Music*

(Los Angeles)
*Crashed*
*Little Elvises*
*The Fame Thief*
*Herbie's Game*
*King Maybe*
*Fields Where They Lay*
*Nighttown*
*Rock of Ages*

**METTE IVIE HARRISON**
(Mormon Utah)
*The Bishop's Wife*
*His Right Hand*
*For Time and All Eternities*
*Not of This Fold*
*The Prodigal Daughter*

**MICK HERRON**
(England)
*Slow Horses*
*Dead Lions*
*The List* (A Novella)
*Real Tigers*
*Spook Street*
*London Rules*
*The Marylebone Drop*
  (A Novella)
*Joe Country*
*The Catch* (A Novella)
*Slough House*
*Bad Actors*

*Down Cemetery Road*
*The Last Voice You Hear*
*Why We Die*
*Smoke and Whispers*

*Reconstruction*
*Nobody Walks*
*This Is What Happened*
*Dolphin Junction: Stories*
*The Secret Hours*

**NAOMI HIRAHARA**
(Japantown)
*Clark and Division*
*Evergreen*

**STEPHEN MACK JONES**
(Detroit)
*August Snow*
*Lives Laid Away*
*Dead of Winter*
*Deus X*

**LENE KAABERBØL & AGNETE FRIIS**
(Denmark)
*The Boy in the Suitcase*
*Invisible Murder*
*Death of a Nightingale*
*The Considerate Killer*

**MARTIN LIMÓN**
(South Korea)
*Jade Lady Burning*
*Slicky Boys*
*Buddha's Money*
*The Door to Bitterness*
*The Wandering Ghost*
*G.I. Bones*
*Mr. Kill*
*The Joy Brigade*
*Nightmare Range*
*The Iron Sickle*
*The Ville Rat*
*Ping-Pong Heart*
*The Nine-Tailed Fox*
*The Line*
*GI Confidential*
*War Women*

**ED LIN**
(Taiwan)
*Ghost Month*
*Incensed*
*99 Ways to Die*
*Death Doesn't Forget*

**PETER LOVESEY**
(England)
*The Circle*
*The Headhunters*
*False Inspector Dew*
*Rough Cider*
*On the Edge*
*The Reaper*

(Bath, England)
*The Last Detective*
*Diamond Solitaire*
*The Summons*
*Bloodhounds*
*Upon a Dark Night*

**PETER LOVESEY CONT.**
*The Vault*
*Diamond Dust*
*The House Sitter*
*The Secret Hangman*
*Skeleton Hill*
*Stagestruck*
*Cop to Corpse*
*The Tooth Tattoo*
*The Stone Wife*
*Down Among the Dead Men*
*Another One Goes Tonight*
*Beau Death*
*Killing with Confetti*
*The Finisher*
*Diamond and the Eye*
*Showstopper*

(London, England)
*Wobble to Death*
*The Detective Wore*
  *Silk Drawers*
*Abracadaver*
*Mad Hatter's Holiday*
*The Tick of Death*
*A Case of Spirits*
*Swing, Swing Together*
*Waxwork*

*Bertie and the Tinman*
*Bertie and the Seven Bodies*
*Bertie and the Crime of Passion*

**SUJATA MASSEY**
(1920s Bombay)
*The Widows of Malabar Hill*
*The Satapur Moonstone*
*The Bombay Prince*
*The Mistress of Bhatia House*

**FRANCINE MATHEWS**
(Nantucket)
*Death in the Off-Season*
*Death in Rough Water*
*Death in a Mood Indigo*
*Death in a Cold Hard Light*
*Death on Nantucket*
*Death on Tuckernuck*
*Death on a Winter Stroll*

**SEICHŌ MATSUMOTO**
(Japan)
*Inspector Imanishi*
  *Investigates*

**CHRIS McKINNEY**
(Post Apocalyptic Future)
*Midnight, Water City*
*Eventide, Water City*
*Sunset, Water City*

**PHILIP MILLER**
(North Britain)
*The Goldenacre*

**FUMINORI NAKAMURA**
(Japan)
*The Thief*
*Evil and the Mask*
*Last Winter, We Parted*
*The Kingdom*
*The Boy in the Earth*
*Cult X*
*My Annihilation*
*The Rope Artist*

**STUART NEVILLE**
(Northern Ireland)
*The Ghosts of Belfast*
*Collusion*
*Stolen Souls*
*The Final Silence*
*Those We Left Behind*

*So Say the Fallen*

*The Traveller & Other Stories*
*House of Ashes*

(Dublin)
*Ratlines*

**KWEI QUARTEY**
(Ghana)
*Murder at Cape Three Points*
*Gold of Our Fathers*
*Death by His Grace*

*The Missing American*
*Sleep Well, My Lady*
*Last Seen in Lapaz*

**NILIMA RAO**
(1910s Fiji)
*A Disappearance in Fiji*

**MARCIE R. RENDON**
(Minnesota's Red River Valley)
*Murder on the Red River*
*Girl Gone Missing*
*Sinister Graves*

**JAMES SALLIS**
(New Orleans)
*The Long-Legged Fly*
*Moth*
*Black Hornet*
*Eye of the Cricket*
*Bluebottle*
*Ghost of a Flea*

*Sarah Jane*

**MICHAEL SEARS**
(Queens, New York)
*Tower of Babel*

**JOHN STRALEY**
(Sitka, Alaska)
*The Woman Who Married a Bear*
*The Curious Eat Themselves*
*The Music of What Happens*
*Death and the Language
    of Happiness*
*The Angels Will Not Care*
*Cold Water Burning*
*Baby's First Felony*
*So Far and Good*

(Cold Storage, Alaska)
*The Big Both Ways*
*Cold Storage, Alaska*
*What Is Time to a Pig?*
*Blown by the Same Wind*

**LEONIE SWANN**
(England)
*The Sunset Years of Agnes Sharp*

**KAORU TAKAMURA**
(Japan)
*Lady Joker*

**CAMILLA TRINCHIERI**
(Tuscany)
*Murder in Chianti*
*The Bitter Taste of Murder*
*Murder on the Vine*

**HELENE TURSTEN**
(Sweden)
*Detective Inspector Huss*
*The Torso*
*The Glass Devil*
*Night Rounds*
*The Golden Calf*
*The Fire Dance*
*The Beige Man*

**HELENE TURSTEN CONT.**
*The Treacherous Net*
*Who Watcheth*
*Protected by the Shadows*

*Hunting Game*
*Winter Grave*
*Snowdrift*

*An Elderly Lady Is Up
    to No Good*
*An Elderly Lady Must Not
    Be Crossed*

**ILARIA TUTI**
(Italy)
*Flowers over the Inferno*
*The Sleeping Nymph*
*Daughter of Ashes*

**JACQUELINE WINSPEAR**
(1920s England)
*Maisie Dobbs*
*Birds of a Feather*